HIS WILL BE DONE . . .

"What do you want, Estelle?" Steve said.

"Barney's estate is worth two million dollars, Steve. I want it! But the son of a bitch changed his will. He cut me out of it, Steve. Me, his wife. Here, I'll show you."

"I, BARNEY STREET, being of sound and disposing mind, memory and understanding, do hereby make, publish and declare this to be my Last Will and Testament . . . I give, devise and bequeath all the rest, residue and remainder of my estate, both real and personal of every nature, wherever situated and whenever acquired, of which I may die seized or possessed, to Milo Hacha. . . ."

Steve stopped reading. "Who the hell is Milo Hacha?"

"The man you're going to kill!"

Other SIGNET Ellery Queen Titles

Dead Man's Tale

by

ELLERY QUEEN

A SIGNET BOOK from
NEW AMERICAN LIBRARY
TIMES MIRROR

Contents

Part ONE

Barney

———◆———

1

Steve Longacre wheeled his convertible out of Neck Road and into the long driveway delicately.

Here goes nobody.

And, this is where I came in.

He glanced up at the sky and to his surprise it was purely blue, with the spring sun blazing. He shivered.

He drove the several hundred yards to the gate with great care. He braced himself and touched his horn.

Right away he heard the reception committee. Pete Taurasi appeared beyond the high cyclone fence with the damn Dobermans, a brace of black-and-buff killers lunging against their heavy steel leashes.

"If it ain't Mr. Longacre," Pete said warmly.

"How's by you, Petey?" Steve said, watching the dogs.

"Like as usual," Petey said, setting the Dobermans back on their haunches. They sat there, watching Steve. "You look in the pink."

"You know me, Petey. A real cool cat."

Petey Taurasi laughed, showing his brown fangs. Good old Petey, Steve thought. Dog manure on his shoes and a hearty case of halitosis. "Don't say cat around here, Mr. Longacre," Petey said. "These pups take it personal." He unlocked the gate and yanked the dogs away. "Go right on up. She's expecting you."

The convertible spewed gravel as Steve swung around the

circular driveway. Behind him he could hear Taurasi, still laughing.

He brought his car to a jarring stop before Barney Street's proudest possession but one. The monstrosity of a Tudor mansion was even uglier than Steve remembered it. He got out and turned around and there she was, draped in the doorway.

Barney Street's proudest possession but none.

"Steve," she said. She held out her hand.

"Hello, Estelle."

"My, aren't we formal," the woman said, smiling. "Come on in."

Steve followed her into the enormous house, his eyes on the exposed V of her tanned velvet back. He had to hand it to Estelle. She was still built. And the way she walked. No twitching her hips in your face. Girly-girly, like a teen-ager. She must be thirty-five, Steve thought. Maybe more.

She went straight to the bar at the far end of the long, cool living room.

The high ceiling was open-beamed, the walls oak-paneled. The rosewood concert grand stood in the bulging bay window overlooking the Sound. There were a few new paintings on the walls—crazy stuff, all blots and drips, as if an army of bugs had got into some paint pots and tried to wipe their feet off on the canvas. The field-stone fireplace had a hearth almost as broad as the piano.

"What are you drinking these days, Stevie?" Estelle asked, still turned away from him.

Steve said he was drinking bourbon. Ice tinkled. He watched Estelle's bare brown arms, firm-fleshed and young-looking. He felt a sudden trickle of sweat leave an icy trail down his side.

When she swung about there was the old gamin smile on her lips. Fixed, as if she had had some trouble putting it on. Her eyes, more darkly smudged than he remembered, told a different story. They were cautious and excited at the same time.

She walked over and handed Steve a glass. "The least I expected from my old playmate was a little kiss," she said. She leaned forward, parting her lips. Her summer frock, low-cut, co-operated. "Steve? Stevie?"

"What do you want, Estelle?" Steve said. "Real grief?"

"Don't tell me you're scared of Barney, darlin'," she said, moving closer.

Steve stepped back. "You're damn right I am." He raised his glass, telling himself he was going to sip like a little gentleman. "I don't know why I came," he complained. "I ought to have my head examined."

That did it. She straightened up, her lips hardening. "What head?" she said. Steve watched the big freeze settle over her, solving his problem, and he gratefully downed the bourbon. She stalked over to the sofa and flung herself back on it, tucked one leg under her and started swinging the other. They were short vicious swings. "You came because I told you to. You had no choice at all. Now did you, Steve?"

He couldn't think of an answer. He turned to the big picture window and looked out at the Sound, studying the little white scraps of sail bobbing around on it.

"Turn around, you ape, when I'm talking to you."

Steve turned around.

"They're going to kill him," Estelle said.

"What?"

"You're dumb, but you're not that dumb. You know it, I know it, everybody knows it."

Steve went over to the bar and poured himself an unhealthy slug. "So what?" he said casually. "Let Barney put his running shoes on."

"He couldn't run that far," Estelle said. It was really remarkable how cold that girly voice could get. "And neither could you."

"Me?" Steve said. "I don't have to run."

"Not now you don't," Estelle said. "But that could change, Stevie."

"Thanks for reminding me."

"Besides," Estelle said, looking into her glass, "he couldn't run away if he tried."

"What's to stop him?"

Estelle smiled. She set her glass down on the floor and said, "Steve, I want you to do something for me."

"Damn it, Estelle. You're poison to me!"

She got up and came over, very close. "Don't shout, lover. You're in no position to shout at me."

"Okay! Okay. . . ."

"Barney found out about us," Estelle said.

"My God!" Steve said.

"Oh, it's all right—"

"All *right!*"

"I tell you, it's all right. The important thing is, they've got their hands on Barney's deposition."

Steve stared at her. "How in hell did they manage to do that?"

"Hurley sold it to them."

"Hurley?"

"His own lawyer." Estelle laughed. "Pretty, isn't it?"

"I don't get it," Steve said. "Why doesn't Barney just put it down on paper again?"

"Because," Estelle said, "he can't."

Steve wondered why Barney Street couldn't put it down on paper again, but he didn't press it. "Anyway, what could I do to help Barney?"

"I didn't say anything about helping Barney. You weren't listening. I said he found out how it used to be between us. I want you to help me."

"But that's—" Steve groped for a word "—ancient history."

"Not to Barney it wasn't. I don't know how he found out. He found out. Maybe Taurasi told him. What difference does it make? He knew he was going to die and he found out about us. He beat me up." Estelle shrugged; then she added, "The son of a bitch changed his will."

Steve didn't say anything.

"He cut me out of it, Steve. Me, his wife. Out in the cold. Do you like what you've got?"

Steve didn't know what he was supposed to say. "I guess so."

"Well, I like what I've got. Barney's estate is worth two million dollars, Steve. Two . . . million . . . bucks. I want it. I want to keep it. Here, I'll show you his will."

Steve watched her leave the room, surprised that she had access to Barney's will. She returned in a few moments with a document bound in pale-blue paper. Steve unfolded it.

I, BARNEY STREET, residing at 14 Neck Road, The Neck, Long Island, New York, being of sound and disposing mind, memory and understanding, do hereby make, publish and declare this to be my Last Will and Testament, hereby revoking any and all codicils by me at any time heretofore made.

FIRST: I direct that all my just debts and funeral expenses be paid as soon after my decease as may be practicable.

SECOND: I give, devise and bequeath all the rest, residue and remainder of my estate, both real and personal of every nature, wherever situated and whenever acquired, of which I may die seized or possessed, to Milo Hacha, whose last known residence was Oosterdijk, the Netherlands. . . .

There was more, but Steve stopped reading. "Who the hell," he asked, "is Milo Hacha?"

"Late in 1943," Estelle murmured, "Barney bailed out of a crippled B-17 over the Dutch countryside."

"That was eighteen years ago," Steve protested.

"A man named Milo Hacha, an N.C.O. with the German army of occupation in Holland, saved Barney's life. In eighteen years he hasn't stopped talking about it."

"A German?" Steve was confused. He hadn't expected this. He hadn't expected anything like it. "Besides, Milo Hacha's no German name."

"He was a Czech. In the German army. He turned on the Nazis," Estelle said, "helping Allied airmen, working in the Dutch underground. The way Barney told it, Hacha practically liberated Holland singlehanded. Every time Barney got mellow over a few drinks, he talked about Hacha. After the war, he even sent the guy CARE packages every month. That went on for a year and a half, maybe two years. Hacha had stayed on in Holland, you see. Then, all of a sudden, CARE said they couldn't locate Hacha. He'd just dropped out of sight."

"Still on his uppers?"

"I don't know. Barney even had a British private dick try to find Hacha. He took Barney's cabled retainer and never sent a report. Barney cabled him a couple of times, then forgot about it." Estelle went over to the piano and ran a finger down the keys, ending with a thud in the bass. "CARE packages!" She looked at Steve. "Two million bucks. My money, Steve. I want it."

"Barney isn't even dead yet."

Estelle ignored him. "You didn't read far enough. It's all spelled out. How Barney wants his executor to spend any amount of money and time to find Hacha."

"Will it stand up in court?"

"Hurley says . . ."

"Hurley?" It was barely a question. Nothing surprised him now.

"Go ahead, try to make something out of it. I said I want that money."

Then Steve made a mistake. "You'd go to Hurley, after what he did?"

Estelle slapped his face, hard. "There's another deposition —which I could sign. Don't forget it!"

"Barney was my friend," Steve said, touching his cheek. He wondered why he was speaking of Barney, as Estelle was, in the past tense.

"Why didn't you think of that when you were making love to me while Barney was off fighting for dear old Uncle Sam?" Estelle asked, smiling sweetly. "Where I get my help is my business. Now I'm getting it from you."

"What do you want from me?" Steve asked, well remembering that smile.

"I just want you to go to Europe for me," she said. "Find Hacha and come back to tell me he's dead."

"What if he isn't dead?"

"I want you to go to Europe for me," Estelle repeated, distinctly. "And come back to tell me he's dead."

Steve stood very still. "You've gone nuts," he said.

"Not I." Estelle had stopped smiling. "I haven't gone nuts, as you put it. But come on upstairs and see who has."

Steve opened his mouth. Then he shut it and followed her.

Barney's room was on the north side of the house, facing the Sound. It had a large French door pierced by spears of sun ricocheting off the water. A figure stood before it, but all Steve could see against the glare was the man's short, blocky silhouette.

"Estelle?"

"Barney, you have a visitor."

Barney turned around. "Steve, you son of a gun!" he cried in a childish voice. "How the hell are you?"

Steve could smell him. He needed a shave and a haircut. His slacks were rumpled and stained. He moved sloppily, as if all his muscles had collapsed. He had put on a lot of weight. He was a fat man. And he smelled.

As they shook hands, Steve felt Barney's—limp and damp.

"You know what, Stevie?" Barney said excitedly. "I'm getting out. For good. You think I'm kidding?"

Steve mumbled something.

"Hurley says I can do it. They wouldn't dare touch an ex-fixer, Stevie. You can see they wouldn't dare, huh? Not even Harry Craven. Not none of them. I'll have the last laugh, Stevie boy. Don't think I won't. 'Put it all down in black and white and I'll keep it for you if we need it,' Hurley says. He's one right guy. Then if Craven's got any bitching to do, he can just choke on it. I should worry. Huh, Stevie?"

"Sure, Barney. Sure," Steve said.

"So I made a mistake," Barney said jovially. "One lousy mistake in ten years. For a fixer that's not a bad score, huh, Stevie? One mistake, and Craven takes a fall for conspiracy. Didn't he know he was in a risky line of work?" Barney chuckled. "Well, maybe it'll do him some good to take a fall. When he gets out he might have some—what they say?—humility."

"Craven's been out for six months now," Steve mentioned.

"What? You don't know what you're talking about. They gave him five to ten, Steve, remember? That's plenty of time to burn your bridges. Why, just the other day I saw Hack Northy, and . . ."

The voice went on, childish, enthusiastic. Hack Northy, a hood in the county strong-arm squad, had lost his face by a shotgun blast on a New York street corner four years before.

Steve listened to Barney Street's new voice and tried not to smell Barney Street's new smell. He didn't know what to say or do. Barney was babbling. He'd gone nuts, as Estelle had said. But that must have happened after he wrote his new will. Otherwise Estelle wouldn't have had a thing to worry about. And I wouldn't be here now, Steve thought. He wanted, suddenly, to be somewhere else. Anywhere. He couldn't stand to see Barney like this.

"I got to be going now," Steve said.

"No, Stevie! Stick around, Steve, will you please?"

"Barney, honest. I got to be going."

Barney's face screwed up in a comical grimace of disappointment. "Well, if you got to. I'll walk you to the door."

Steve thought he meant the entrance downstairs, but Barney went only as far as the doorway of his bedroom. He peered cautiously into the hall, looking both ways, then quickly pulled his head back inside. "Come see me again soon, Stevie," he said. "You're always welcome here. Make him one for the road, Estelle."

Estelle said she would. Steve followed her downstairs.

In the living room Steve asked, "How long has he been like this, Estelle?"

"Ever since Harry Craven was paroled. Why?"

"Because with his deposition in their possession and the way he is now, he couldn't testify against them. What's the big tumult? They'd be crazy to touch a hair of his head."

"That is," Estelle said, "if they knew."

"Then tell them."

"And how about me? The head-shrinker calls it regression. Barney can't face what he's got to face, so he crawls back into kiddieland where everything is nice and safe. You think I want to be saddled with that? He won't leave his room. I practically have to take him to the bathroom."

"Then have him committed."

"Don't tell me what to do, Steve, I'm doing this my way."

"And I thought you said he found out about us," Steve said suddenly.

"He found out. But back where he is now he hasn't found out. Back where he is now, he doesn't even know he's going to die."

"You bitch," Steve said. "You want them to kill him."

Estelle's eyes shrank to steel points. "He knew about us for almost six months before this happened. He treated me like dirt. He let me know about the will. He crowed about it. He even gave me a copy. He made me read it every night before we went to bed."

"So you had a talk with Hurley?"

Estelle ignored his question. "Do you have a passport, Steve?"

"Why would I want a passport?"

"Get one. I'm not kidding, Steve. If you think I'm kidding, read the papers in the morning."

"The papers?" Steve said blankly.

"In the morning. Then get a passport. Then go to Europe and come back to tell me how Milo Hacha died."

Estelle crossed the living room and went down the hall to the front door. She opened the door, said, "Good-by,

Steve." Cupping her hands around her mouth, she called out, "Petey! Watch the dogs. Steve's going home."

Steve went through the doorway.

"Bon voyage," Estelle said pleasantly.

———◆———

2

Andy Longacre pulled the MG into the driveway, almost hoping Steve would be out. He wanted to think. That was odd; he had had four years in which to think. Four surprisingly good years, because at first he had been deadset against going to college.

But he had used those four years to explore himself, his new and utterly unexpected self, and to explore a world the old Andy Longacre had not even known existed. From black motorcycle jacket and garrison belt with filed-down buckle to B.A. in Comparative Language and Literature and Phi Beta Kappa Key in four years. *Wunderbar!* And now?

He saw Steve's car in the garage, shrugged and unstrapped his big, battered suitcase from the MG's rack. Maybe, he thought, I should have studied accounting. If I had I'd be able to help my brother spend the money he's earned as right-hand man to Long Island County's ex-Mr. Fixit. Besides, if I'd studied accounting I wouldn't be mixed up now.

The trouble was that the new Andy Longacre, born some time during the past four years, had been weaned on literature and philosophy and . . . oh, hell, leave us not exhume David Hume. Andy smiled.

Damned gold-plated snob, he muttered to himself. Who the hell are you to judge your brother?

Andy lugged his suitcase up the walk toward the front porch. The grass needed mowing and the porch railing could stand a coat of paint. He'd take care of the lawn first thing after unpacking and maybe having a drink with Steve. He didn't feel at all tired in spite of having driven all night and most of the day, with only two stops along the way to eat.

He was a tall, rangy youth. He had crew-cut sandy hair

and wore shell-rimmed glasses for reading and driving. And
although he hadn't really pushed it, the coeds at the big
Midwestern university had been more than co-operative. He
was twenty-two and healthy and had nowhere to go.

And his brother was a crook.

Andy found Steve in the living room, stretched out limply
on the sofa, his face gray, his striped suit a mess. There was
a trace of spittle on his heavy lips and a strong odor of
bourbon.

He tried to make Steve sit up. "Come on, boy. Come on,
we'll put you to bed." But Steve's body was limp and un-
responsive. Andy decided to leave him there. He removed
Steve's shoes and covered him with a blanket. That was
when Steve decided to get sick. Andy went for a washrag
and a pan of cold water. Home-sweet-home, he thought.

Then Andy frowned. Steve had never been much of a
drinker, certainly not a solo drinker guzzling himself stupid
on a sunny afternoon.

Andy sat down and smoked a cigarette. He looked at his
suitcase with the Big-Ten stickers, faded and torn, on the
worn cowhide. Steve had given him the suitcase as a going-
away present when he'd left for college. Since then it had
seen bumper service, bouncing back and forth Christmas and
Easter and summer vacations between the Midwest and Long
Island. Steve had appeared noticeably older and less sure of
himself each time Andy had come home.

Even during that time Barney Street had been finished,
and so was Steve. Andy knew the history; he had even gotten an obscure satisfaction in using it as the basis of a term
paper in an elective criminology course he had taken in his
junior year. He had called the paper "The Old-Style Fixer
and the New in County Crime."

Barney Street and his lieutenant, Steve Longacre, were old-
style fixers. There were those who claimed that Street's
failure to keep Harry Craven out of jail for conspiracy in the
county labor-war maiming of a crusading reporter had started
Barney's long slide downward, but Barney had been doomed
in any case. Barney Street was an old-style fixer, and the end
had been inevitable.

The new-style fixer was a lawyer who used a low-handicap
golf game and cocktail-party manners the way Barney Street
had used strong-arm goons and the outmoded tactics of the
Prohibition mobs.

The up-to-date fixer eschewed the hard threat, the schlamin with a sawed-off length of iron pipe or rubber hose and the artillery. For these he substituted a complex *modus operandi* the Barney Streets were incapable of understanding. Andy's term paper described this *modus operandi* in clinical detail.

With the same perversity that had made him write the paper, Andy had shown it to Steve. He had watched Steve's face while his brother read it. Steve's face hadn't told Andy anything, but when he put the paper down he had said, "This is what I send you to college for?"

"I just want your opinion, that's all," Andy had said defensively.

Steve only thumped him on the back, laughing hard. "You're all right, kid. Getting to be a real professor. But why don't you write about Shakespeare and stuff like that, and leave my racket to the guys who understand it?"

Andy had never mentioned the subject again.

Steve started making funny noises in his throat. His eyelids fluttered and he tried to sit up.

"If I tell Craven," he said.

"What?" Andy said.

"If I tell Craven," Steve said again. He sat up, his eyes opening wide. Then he lurched into the bathroom. He came back in a few minutes with water dripping from his hair and face and his jacket soaked.

"Hello, kid," he said. "This is a great way to welcome you home." He ran his big hands through his hair, looking Andy over. "Phi Bete, huh? How about that?" But his thoughts were obviously elsewhere.

"What's the matter, Steve?"

"The matter? Nothing's the matter." Steve sat down heavily on the sofa.

"You mumbled something about Craven."

"To hell with Craven. All of them," Steve muttered.

Andy watched him. "I've been thinking. I've had an offer of a fellowship out on the West Coast. To do my graduate work. Why not pack up and come along, Steve? There's nothing keeping you here."

Steve didn't look up. "Me, run away? You must be rocky."

"I didn't say anything about running away."

Then Steve did look up. His face was haggard. "I don't

. . . " His voice faltered. His eyes squinched shut and it took Andy a moment to realize he was crying. Steve turned away. "Go on," he said harshly. "Go on, get out of here and buy us a steak or something! We'll celebrate. Andy, get out, will you? Give me a couple of minutes, please!"

"If there's anything—"

"God damn it, get out!"

Andy got up and left.

They're going to kill him, Steve thought. They're going to rub out Barney Street for no reason except that the bitch wants them to.

Gutless wonder, Steve said to himself. That's what you are!

He reached for the bottle, but what whisky was left made him gag.

Gutless wonder. . . .

Because you're not going to do a damn thing about it.

There were only three things Estelle Street had to do that night after Petey Taurasi went into Huntington to see a sexy movie, and all three were apple pie. First, to make sure that the front gate wasn't locked. Second, to see that the gate to the Dobermans' run *was* locked. Third . . .

Estelle went down the wooden stairs that hugged the bluff overlooking the Sound. It was a warm, windless night. She slipped out of her terry-cloth robe and stood for a moment on the sand, watching the moonlight dapple the water with silver.

This would be her first swim of the season. The water would be cold, but afterward the thick robe would cuddle her. Estelle loved to swim. She liked it best when the water was cold and her nipples puckered and stiffened. It was best when she was swimming alone, in the night, naked.

She looked back once at the high-gabled house on the bluff, a cutout in black paper against the moonlighted sky. Some house! she thought. Charles Addams would go wild over it. Barney had started with a small Tudor-type building and had added and added to it, endlessly. Good old Barney, Estelle thought. Good old loud, tasteless, big-hearted slob. You were great when you had it. But now . . .

She said a four-letter word aloud, repeated it, said it a third time. As if it reminded her of something, she looked down at herself with enjoyment, ran her hands over her flanks, gleaming in the moonlight. Then she walked into the Sound.

The water was cold, so cold it made her gasp with delight. She swam a few strokes, rolled over on her back.

She thought she heard a car somewhere above the beach. Not far. On the bluff.

Estelle did a whirlabout in a shower of silver drops and with a smooth, fast crawl swam out into deep water.

The car stopped on the circular driveway and two men got out. The big one wore slacks and a sports shirt with the collar laid back. The other was little and skinny and wore a dark-blue suit. The big man, who had been driving, left the motor idling. The two men stood quietly for a moment, listening to the Dobermans.

"I'm not wild about this," the little man said.

The big man shrugged. "They're locked up. You worry too much."

"I just don't like them dogs," the little man insisted. "I heard all about Barney Street's dogs."

"You're a regular old lady," the big man said. "Come on."

The front door was not locked. There was a light on in the hall and another on the stairway landing. The high-pile carpet in the hall and on the stairs muffled their footfalls. They went up side by side, not hurrying.

"Estelle?" a voice above them called. "Wasn't that a car?"

They reached the top of the stairs and turned left. There were two dark doorways and one door partly open with light behind it. They went to the partly open door and heard someone shuffling around beyond it.

"Estelle?" The door started to close.

The big man raised his foot and kicked it open.

Barney Street stood there, a silly smile on his face.

The big man shot the smile off his face three times with a .45. The little man shot him in the belly once with a snub Police Positive. When Barney Street fell down he didn't look much like anything any more.

The two men went down the stairs. Out of the house, they climbed into their car. The big man drove it sedately around the circular driveway, heading for the gate. The dogs were still barking.

When Estelle saw the headlights swing out onto the road, she rolled over again and began to swim slowly back to shore. The cold water made her tingle all over, especially her breasts. She felt wonderful.

Part TWO

Old Joost

---◆---

3

Mynheer Van Hilversum stared angrily at the neat stack of papers on his desk.

They were all there—the police records from the war years and afterward; the yellowed sheets of the underground newspaper; the dozen or so occupation orders that had been rescued from the fire in the town hall that mad summer in 1944—some of them bearing Milo Hacha's extravagant signature.

Mynheer Van Hilversum was a completely bald, fusty little man who wore rimless glasses that were always sliding down his bridgeless nose. He had an enormous drooping mustache that had been the color of corn silk in 1944. Now it was white.

For twenty-odd years he had been the mayor of Oosterdijk, where everything but the big dredging machines that were transforming the old Zuider Zee into fertile polder land stood still. Twenty-some years this past April, he thought with a sigh.

He neatly rearranged the papers a third time, lining them up precisely with the edge of his desk. If he got to his feet and looked past the heavy, comfortable furniture and through the window across the room he could see the Oosterdijk Canal running straight, like a ruler, across the flat, green countryside to Hoorn. He could also see, far down the canal, the sails of Old Joost's windmill stubbornly turning in defiance of the electric water-pumping stations. But Mynheer Van Hilversum did not wish to see Old Joost's windmill, so he did not look out the window.

"Tell them about the girl," his wife said.

The mayor looked up. He had forgotten she was there. "That is out of the question, Johanna."

"Tell them about the girl!"

"I will never tell them about the girl," Hilversum said, shaking his head.

"You old fool, if you don't tell them, I will."

Johanna was a big woman, with a blocky red face and blond hair going gray. She had been strappingly pretty in 1944. Mynheer Van Hilversum, though he had been mayor for almost a quarter of a century, had always been a little afraid of her.

She leaned over the desk and riffled contemptuously through the papers Hilversum had stacked there. "These?" she sniffed. "What are these? Do they tell the whole story?"

Hilversum admitted they did not. He took a large watch out of his vest pocket and fussed with it, wishing the Americans would return soon so he could have done with the whole sorry business. "Sergeant Hacha was a member of the occupation army," he said patiently. "But Sergeant Hacha was a Czech who did not like his German masters. So—"

"At least you can speak his name now," Johanna interrupted. "It's years since you have spoken his name."

"Please, Johanna," her husband pleaded.

"I could not help doing what I did! I am not ashamed!"

Hilversum's close-set little eyes blinked. "No, I suppose you couldn't. I don't blame you, Johanna. I blame no one."

"And the Englishman?"

"I know nothing of the Englishman."

Johanna laughed. When she stopped laughing, she pointed a large finger at Hilversum. "The two Americans spoke of a legacy. Since Milo Hacha is dead, that legacy belongs to the girl. I want her to have it."

Hilversum scrubbed his face with dry hands. It was a mannerism his wife detested. His glasses fell off and landed on the desk. He retrieved them and set about polishing them with a large handkerchief. "They will want information about the mother."

"I am not ashamed."

"*I* am."

Johanna shrugged. "Why should we have to stay here in Oosterdijk? If Katrina Joost received the legacy, we could go anywhere."

"So now it comes out," Hilversum said, sighing. "It is the money you want."

"Katrina Joost is the rightful heiress."

"And you are the rightful guardian."

"Well, am I not?" There was a faint knock at the door.

"The Americans," Johanna whispered. "You'll tell them?"

"No," Hilversum said.

Hans appeared. "Mynheer, the Americans are here."

"In a moment."

The servant, whom Mynheer Van Hilversum could barely afford, nodded and withdrew.

"Your own wife's flesh and blood," Johanna said venomously. "And you wish her to spend her life with that dirty old blind man?"

"Old Joost is dying," Hilversum said, although he knew that changed nothing for the better.

"And he will leave Katrina, when he dies, a creaky old windmill and a run-down farm! Remember, Mynheer. If you don't tell *hem—*"

"Hans!" Hilversum called. He looked at his wife. "And now, get out."

He was almost surprised when she obeyed.

The older of the two Americans came in first, said something in his difficult language, smiled and stuck out his hand. Mynheer Van Hilversum assumed he was supposed to shake the outthrust hand, so he did. The younger American, hardly more than a boy, said in a French Hilversum could understand, "We appreciate the trouble you've gone to for us, Monsieur."

Hilversum waved deprecatingly and answered in French, "It is nothing. Will you please be seated?"

Steve and Andy Longacre sat down. Hans came into the room with a tray of cheese and bread and beer. Steve, looking with distrust at the mottled headcheese, selected a slice of Edam. "Ask him if we can have the papers we want photostated, Andy. Unless you think that's rushing things."

"How should I know?" Andy said in English, and asked the question in French.

Hilversum nodded at once. "But of course. As mayor of

Oosterdijk, I can even certify the copies for you. Will that
be satisfactory?"

"The old boy seems in a hurry," Steve said after Andy
had translated.

"Isn't that what you want?"

"I guess so. Tell him we want to know how Milo Hacha
died."

"Your friend back home is going to be disappointed,"
Andy said.

"What? Oh. Sure. Well, that's the way it goes."

Andy translated the request and Hilversum nodded again.
He spent the next few minutes shuffling through the mis-
cellany on his desk, withdrawing old newspapers, mimeo-
graphed forms, a police report.

"These are in German," he said, "except for the underground newspapers." He added with unforgotten bitterness,
"Even our police reports were in German in those days. You
read German?"

"Yes, I do," Andy said. "We'll have them photostated and
then return them at once if that's all right with you."

"But of course, Monsieur."

Andy and Steve shook hands with the mayor and asked
if they could see him tomorrow. Hilversum said that he
would be honored. Hans materialized to show them out.

The mayor's strapping wife, who the Americans assumed
was twenty years younger than Hilversum, was waiting by
the front door. She smiled at Steve and Andy. "You have
what you wish?" she asked in French.

Andy nodded.

Just then Hilversum came down the hall, staring unhap-
pily at his wife. But she smiled at Andy, looked outside and
said, "It will rain soon, Messieurs." She spoke a stilted school-
book French. "There is nothing more dismal than Oosterdijk
in the rain."

Andy saw dark clouds brooding over the low banks of the
canal. The red-brick sidewalk was almost gray in the dreary
light. Down-canal, past the streets of the little town, black
and white cows were drinking peacefully.

Hilversum shook hands with them again. Once Andy
thought the old man glared at his wife. The woman shook
their hands, too, with crushing enthusiasm.

"Thank you for your hospitality, Vrouw Van Hilversum,"
Andy said, wishing she would let go.

Then, with a shock, he realized that she was pressing something into his hand—a folded piece of paper. Andy palmed it and slipped it into his pocket as he followed Steve out. Could the mayor's Amazonian wife have developed a sudden yen for him? He hoped that the smile he was directing at old Hilversum over his shoulder was not as guilty-looking as it felt.

Her prediction had been right, for the sky opened up suddenly. They had to run back to the hotel through a driving rain.

4

From Andy Longacre's diary:

. . . when he read in the papers that Barney Street had been murdered, sure he was scared. Who wouldn't be? He was Street's lieutenant. But the way Steve was scared was something I hated to see. Maybe the picture I'd formed in my mind of Steve when I was a kid had something to do with it. But, I can't blame myself for that, and I can't blame Steve. It just happened.

He was twenty when our parents died in the auto accident, and I was seven. For a long time he tried being father and mother to me, but that isn't the part I remember. The part I remember is carrying his glove to baseball games and cheering myself hoarse when he pitched that no-hitter against Republic. Practically everything I learned came from him.

His getting married must have been part of it. He married young, it fizzled. Looking back on it, I think he got married hoping Joyce would be the mother he thought I needed. But she was no good, and it didn't last three years. Or maybe it didn't last because he was in the rackets even then, I don't know.

Anyhow, I already had my image of Steve and it took a long time to realize it didn't fit the facts. I sure as hell didn't know it before I went off to college, because I wanted to be just like Steve. That's why he sent me out of town, I guess.

He turned white when he read about Barney Street's murder. All of a sudden he looked like a defeated old man and he's only thirty-six. Then, he said he was going to Europe.

"For a friend," he said. "There's this inheritance and it looks like I'm elected to find the heir."

I said I wanted to go with him, but he told me it was out of the question. I didn't ask him why he had to go. Maybe I should have, but looking back on it I must have figured it wasn't a bad idea if he got out of town for a while. Because if they'd killed Street they might be gunning for Street's right-hand man, too.

Also, an overseas trip appealed to me. That part of it was selfish, but I wanted to go. We knocked it around for a while and I finally talked Steve into it by pointing out that I could speak French, German and Russian, while all he could talk was American, and a pretty specialized brand of American at that.

Ten days later we took a KLM flight to The Hague.

Except for a jaunt up to Canada with Steve the year before I got out of high school, this is my first trip out of the United States. Maybe that's why it's difficult to sort out my impressions. Or maybe it's because I'm worried about Steve and still trying to figure out what he's after.

Anyhow, I decided this diary would be a big help, because if I write down what I see and experience, it will stick better. That's what they teach you in college. Funny, I've been out of school less than a month. It seems much longer than that.

The Hague is a beautiful city. They string flowers—geraniums mostly—on wires over the narrow, crooked streets. The Dutch meander along these streets as if they'd never heard of the automobile. It's rough on drivers, but the bikes are even worse. There are millions of them. Kids ride them. Grownups go to work on them. Elderly women in black come whizzing down the streets and young couples pedal along holding hands. There are ten million people in Holland and five million bicycles. At least, that's what they told me at the hotel on Lange Poten Strasse. I believe it.

We didn't stay in The Hague long. We went to the Dutch office of CARE because Steve said they might have something on our man. They did. They brought out the file on Milo Hacha and it showed that Barney Street had been sending monthly packages to Hacha during the early post-war years. Then he just dropped out of existence.

If he was dead, they didn't know it. I couldn't get over the notion that Steve was disappointed. Not because we couldn't find Hacha, but because they couldn't tell him for sure that he was dead. That doesn't make sense, I know, but it's the impression I got.

Unfortunately, the Swiss girl who had handled the Hacha business for CARE isn't with them any more. Her name is Gertrude Ohlendorf and she's gone back to Lucerne. But here is an odd coincidence: she left The Hague a few days after the arrival of Barney Street's last package, the one they couldn't deliver because Hacha had vanished. I guess if it's necessary we can look her up in Lucerne. They gave us her address.

At first it didn't look as if it would be necessary. We took the train to Oosterdijk, where Hacha was stationed during the war. The trip was across country so flat it makes Long Island look like the Alps. Traveling across the countryside like that, you get an idea of how crowded Holland is and how much building is going on here. Except in Oosterdijk, I gather.

Mayor Van Hilversum didn't seem anxious to talk about Milo Hacha at first; then the legacy hooked him. When he heard about that he seemed to get perverse satisfaction in telling us Hacha was dead. And on our second visit he gave us documents establishing Hacha's death beyond any legal doubt.

That seemed to end it and, frankly, I was disappointed. I think I had visions of our wandering all over the face of Europe looking for this mysterious Czech.

Then the mayor's wife dropped her little bombshell. I didn't get a chance to read her note until we returned, drenched, to the hotel. It said: "If you wish to learn more about Milo Hacha, see Old Joost." When she slipped it to me I'd actually thought it was an assignation because of my sex appeal!

While Steve was taking a bath, I went downstairs to the concierge and asked him about Old Joost. Joost is an old blind man, he said, who has a farm about a mile out of town. He lives there with his granddaughter, and I gather he's something of a recluse.

When I went back upstairs I showed Steve the note. He

didn't like it. He'd already been talking about catching the next flight back to the States, and the note jarred him.

We decided, over dinner in the hotel dining room, to see Old Joost first thing in the morning. I must have had a little too much wine, because for no reason at all I blurted out, "Steve, you *wanted* to find out Hacha was dead, didn't you?"

"What do you mean by that, kid?"

"I don't know. I'm asking you." Now that I'd started it, I couldn't stop. "Well, what happens if you find out he's still alive?"

"Alive? You heard the mayor. He's dead. He's dead, kid. Go on upstairs and read the stuff the mayor gave us. It proves Hacha's dead."

"But what about this note?"

"All right. All *right*. I said we'd see this Joost character in the morning, didn't I?"

It had stopped raining, so after dinner I went out for a walk on the red-brick streets of Oosterdijk. I admit it looks as if Milo Hacha is dead. Everything points to it.

But just mentioning the possibility that he's still alive scared Steve as much as reading about Barney Street's murder!

Why?

5

Old Joost liked the sound of the rainwater dripping from the eaves of the old stone farmhouse.

There were other sounds, too, which Old Joost liked: the windmill sails creakily turning as the wind moved them, music to the ears of a man who had spent most of his life in darkness; or the ringing hiss of milk in the metal pails as Katrina emptied the cows' udders, and their contented lowing afterward. But most of all, Katrina's voice as she sang to him after dinner in the farmhouse.

Now Katrina was asleep and there was the sound of the rainwater dripping from the eaves and the faint bubbling in the bowl of his big briar pipe as Old Joost smoked away. The pipe was forbidden, and Old Joost smiled. Heer Doctor Brinker had told Old Joost after the last attack, there would be no more tobacco or he, Brinker, would not be responsible for what happened. So the old man allowed himself one stolen pipeful at night, after Katrina was asleep.

Joost was an angular giant with a leathery face and very large hands which had been once formidable. But now the hands shook; the strength had slipped away. He marveled at his trembling fingers. It hardly seemed possible that with these hands, not too many years ago, he had killed a man.

The man had had a name, but Old Joost no longer remembered it. An Englishman with a wry, clipped accent. His Dutch had been atrocious. He had come to Oosterdijk looking for Milo Hacha. He had not found Hacha, but he was a man of cunning. Because Hacha had once lived with Old Joost at the farmhouse, he had come here. When he had seen Katrina, the Englishman's shrewd mind had gone to work.

Old Joost had been able to tell; the Englishman's voice had changed at the sight of Katrina's dark, kinky hair and her widely-spaced Slavic cheekbones. The blind man had always known what Katrina looked like, all but the coloring; his fingertips had told him.

The Englishman had wanted to take Katrina away. So on a night like this night, with rainwater dripping from the eaves and gusts of wind snapping in the sails of the windmill, Old Joost had killed the Englishman with his hands.

The Englishman had not wanted to die, but Old Joost had not wanted him to take Katrina away, either. The old man remembered the blows the Englishman had rained on his chest and face, but he also remembered the terrible strength in his fingers as they strangled the life out of the stranger. Katrina had been very young then. Had she been in the room? Old Joost just couldn't remember.

He had buried the Englishman behind the windmill. Coming back to the farmhouse, he had stumbled over the dead man's bicycle. So he had dug another hole and buried the bicycle, too, and a few days later Vander Poel, the policeman, had come asking Old Joost about the Englishman, but Old Joost knew nothing.

Joost sighed, wishing he might see—with eyes, not fingers —Katrina's dark, Slavic beauty. But even before she had come to him the Gestapo had destroyed his sight. They had also killed his daughter and his son-in-law because they had been part of the underground that had helped British and American airmen reach the coast and the submarines which took them back to England.

He did not know what had happened to the real Katrina, their child. At first he had accepted the Katrina brought to him by Milo Hacha as his granddaughter. Later, when he realized that the child of his own blood had died with her mother and father in the Gestapo butchery, it no longer mattered. There was only one Katrina.

Until Katrina's seventh birthday a succession of hired girls came to live at the farm, to help in rearing "Joost's granddaughter." There had been frequent visits by the mayor's wife, Johanna, bearing gifts. And for the first three years of Katrina's life Milo Hacha had also come frequently.

It was during those three years that Hilversum had been plotting in secret against the Czech, manufacturing evidence, Joost was certain, to prove that Milo Hacha had been a Nazi criminal. For how could that be? Of all the fighters in the underground the Czech had been the most valuable and courageous, for he worked inside the enemy's camp, in the enemy's own uniform.

Hacha had liked Oosterdijk, and after the war he had settled there. In more ways than one, it was whispered in the town. As for Katrina's true mother, one had only to think of the mayor's wife, with her visits to Joost's farm and her gifts and her concern for the little one's welfare. . . .

Milo Hacha had fled barely in time. Oosterdijk, of course, supposed him to have died. But dead men do not come in the stillness of night, stealthily, to clasp a seven-year-old child in a living embrace and utter a choked good-by.

Katrina had known him as "Uncle" Hacha. Old Joost she had called "Grandfather," as she still did.

He knew what they had begun to say about him, of course. He was getting old, growing soft in the head. He did not mind. It made things easier. His only fear was that Katrina would be taken away from him.

The years passed, and the Englishman had come for Katrina, and Old Joost had strangled him.

Now, on a night like the night he had taken a life, Old Joost sat smoking his pipe, remembering.

A car stopped on the road outside the house.

Old Joost waited motionless on his hard-backed chair. He sat facing the door. He sucked at his pipe once more, but it had gone out. He thought very quickly, confusedly, of his eyes, Milo Hacha, Katrina, the Englishman, Hilversum, Hilversum's wife.

There was a knock at the door.

Only then did Old Joost get up. He went to the door. "Ja?"

"Joost? Let me in."

It was Johanna Hilversum's voice. He unbolted the door and opened it. The night air was cool, with a smell of rain in it. He stepped back. Vrouw Hilversum brushed past him into the room.

"Shut the door," she told Joost.

"I don't like you coming here."

"It is for Katrina's sake. May I sit down?"

"Sit, don't sit. It makes no difference to me." Old Joost shut the door and bolted it.

"There is hardly any air in here. You should open the windows. Katrina—"

"My granddaughter? She is healthy and happy. What do you want?"

"Yesterday two Americans came to Oosterdijk. They are looking for Milo Hacha."

Old Joost felt his heart jump sickeningly. "Milo Hacha is dead!"

"There is a legacy, Joost. A fortune. For Milo Hacha."

"Milo Hacha is *dead*. Doesn't everyone say so?"

"He has an heir."

"Katrina," said Old Joost in a trembling voice, "is my granddaughter."

"Joost. Listen to me. No one wishes to take Katrina away from you."

"You should not have come here. You are not welcome."

"I want Katrina to have that money, Joost."

"She is happy. There is the farm. We work together. She is content. I . . . am used to her."

"You are sick, Joost. Heer Doctor Brinker says—"

"That fool! I will outlive him."

"What will happen to Katrina when you die? Don't you love her?"

"Get out of here," Old Joost said.

"Not until we have talked," Johanna said in a surprisingly gentle voice.

Old Joost turned away. His heart was hammering against his chest. "I told the Americans nothing, I want *you* to tell them. I gave them a note. They are coming here."

"When?" I must be calm, the old man thought. There is real danger again.

"I don't know. Tomorrow, perhaps. You must tell them the truth about Katrina."

"Katrina is my granddaughter. Her parents are dead. They were killed by the Nazis. That is the truth about her."

"You are not the simple-minded old gaffer you pretend to be, Joost. You know well enough who Katrina's real parents are."

"They will never take her from me."

"I've already told you no one wishes to do that. We all want only the best for her."

Old Joost snorted. "Why didn't *you* tell the Americans, then?"

"Because Mynheer Van Hilversum— Coming from you, they would believe. . . . It was you Milo Hacha brought the child to. Her looks alone are not enough, but along with what you could tell them—" The woman, always so self-assured, was actually faltering.

Old Joost filled his pipe, pushing the tobacco down hard with his thumb. He felt strength in his hands now. They were hardly shaking at all. He lit his pipe, put out the match and dropped it on the floor. "When Milo Hacha brought me the child, surely it was with your consent?"

Ah, he had her now. It was coming out, in a stream, a torrent. "No! No! . . . It was right after the war. My husband had gone to Amsterdam. A conference of mayors, concerned with reparations. I was a . . . a big woman, stouter than I am now. I carried the baby without arousing suspicion. When my time approached I went to Hoorn. I could not keep the baby. I knew that.

"Milo Hacha came to Hoorn. When it was safe to do so, he took the child from the midwife's house. I loved my baby. Do you understand that? I loved her! But I let him take her away from me. What else could I do? I was frightened . . . my husband . . . I never dreamed Milo would take the baby back to Oosterdijk."

She was silent. When she spoke again her voice was

steady. "Afterward, when there was talk, he told me. I came here to see the baby, and I knew. Everyone knew. Even Mynheer—but that is nothing, now. You know the way he plotted against Milo Hacha. Why else would he have done that? Milo knew you would provide a home for Katrina. He knew you had lost everything, your whole family—"

"Yes," Old Joost said. "And now Katrina is my whole family."

"Then you will want to do what is best for her. I have never told this story before."

That was true, Old Joost knew. He began to feel fear again.

"So now you know," Johanna said. "Think of me as you wish. Call me whore. But I'm not sorry! If I had the whole thing to do all over again, it would be the same. Will you tell the Americans?"

Old Joost rose, sucking on his pipe. Katrina was asleep in the next room. If he crossed the floor and opened her door he could hear her gentle breathing. He turned toward Johanna Van Hilversum and said one word. "No."

"Old fool—"

"Listen. Listen to me. The girl is my life. Without her I am helpless and empty. I will never give her up. No, don't interrupt. If they come here with their talk of money, what is to stop them from taking her away from me?"

"Simpleton! They won't take her away. And you'll have the money, too!"

"I don't want their money. And you, Johanna? Perhaps you want to claim your child—and get the money for yourself?"

Old Joost waited. When she finally spoke her voice was harsh. "What will you tell them? Because if you don't tell them about Katrina, I will. What will you tell them?"

Old Joost laughed. "I will tell them Milo Hacha is not dead. I will tell them he went away. I will tell them that I saw him after he was supposed to be dead."

"What are you saying?" Johanna cried in a shrill voice.

"That Milo Hacha came to say good-by to the child."

Old Joost felt the woman's strong hands on his shoulders. She was shaking him. "What are you saying?" she cried again.

When he tried to push her away, Old Joost's big hands

found her neck. The pipe fell from his fingers and clattered on the floor.

"Joost!" she managed to cry.

The rainwater dripped from the eaves and there was the familiar creak of the windmill. The old man felt fists beating against his chest and face. This was like choking the Englishman all over again. Now Katrina would be safe. The fists against his chest grew feeble. Then they stopped.

Presently Old Joost went out behind the windmill and dug a hole. Because the ground was wet he could remove the sod in big rectangular chunks matted with grass. The spade splattered him with mud.

When he was finished, he carried her there. He felt a terrible pain in his chest. He stood absolutely still, breathing in gasps. When the pain was gone he buried the Mayor's wife. Groping in the mud on hands and knees, he carefully replaced the sod. Tomorrow he would tell the Americans that Milo Hacha was not dead but had merely gone away.

When he returned to the house, moving heavily, feet dragging, he bumped into the dead woman's car. It was just like the other time, when he had stumbled over the Englishman's bicycle.

But he could not bury a car.

6

The porter at the hotel agreed to drive them to Old Joost's farm and act as interpreter for ten guilders.

"Pretty fancy job," Steve said, indicating the red-and-black Karmann Ghia parked in front of the stone farmhouse.

"But that is not Old Joost's car. Joost cannot drive. That is Mayor Hilversum's car."

"You think his nibs found out about the note?" Steve asked Andy.

"How could he have?"

The porter, still wearing his green apron, pulled his old

Citroën up behind the sleek Karmann Ghia. "Joost!" he called.

A girl came from behind the windmill, leading a cow. She was small and darkly pretty. Perhaps sixteen, Andy thought. She had high cheekbones and pale olive skin. Obviously she was not a native of Oosterdijk. In fact, she looked Slavic.

As she passed, Andy smiled at her. She did not return his smile, but goaded the cow with her stick and walked faster. Just then the door of the farmhouse opened.

An old man appeared in the doorway and shouted something to the girl. Her answer was to goad the cow again and walk still faster. The cowbell clanked. The old man stared straight ahead.

"He's blind, isn't he?" Andy asked the porter.

"Yes. The Nazis did it."

They walked over to the farmhouse. Although Old Joost was a big man, he had once been even bigger, for the shirt and black trousers he wore hung loosely. The stubble of his beard was white, like his hair.

"Who's the girl?" Andy inquired.

"His granddaughter," the porter said in a rather peculiar way. "Katrina." The old man stood aside so they could enter. There was sweat on his face and his head was shaking. He looked sick.

Andy said, "Tell him we'll only take a minute. Tell him we were told he had information about Milo Hacha."

"Hacha?" the porter said in surprise. "But Hacha is dead."

"I'm telling you, it's a wild-goose chase," Steve said.

Andy shrugged. "This is what you wanted, isn't it? To find out about Hacha?"

The porter said something in Dutch. The old man stood motionless, his bluish lips parted, his breath whistling. At last he went directly to a hard-backed chair and sat down. His pale, sightless eyes told nothing. He spoke in a low voice, and what he said seemed to surprise the porter.

"Old Joost says that Milo Hacha is not dead."

"Ask him where Hacha is," Andy said.

"He doesn't know."

Steve frowned. "How the hell does he know the guy's still alive then?"

The porter asked a question and the blind man answered at length. "Once Old Joost did Milo Hacha a favor. Hacha was grateful. Also, right after the war, he lived here for a while. (That is the truth.) They were friends. Then, one day in 1947, Hacha was out on the old Zuider Zee in a fishing boat. There was a storm, and Hacha's boat never returned. No one in Oosterdijk ever saw him again. Everyone believed he had gone down with his boat.

"But now Old Joost claims Hacha came to say good-by to him—afterward. There were those in Oosterdijk who resented Hacha, an ex-German soldier, living among us. They were plotting against him, Old Joost claims. So, Hacha decided to go away. At least, that is what Old Joost claims. Believe it or not, as you wish."

"Why should he lie?" Andy asked.

The porter shrugged. "I did not say he lied. But, except for the girl, he lives alone. He is old. He imagines things."

"Look, kid," Steve said. "It was a crazy idea coming here. We read the stuff the mayor gave us. It tells the same story, about the boat and all. When he certifies the papers they're all the legal proof we'll need that Milo Hacha is dead. Why knock ourselves out over an old nut's pipe dreams?"

"I thought you wanted to find Hacha," Andy said angrily. "It seems to me that if even one man says he's still alive, and since we have the name of the girl who tried to find him for CARE—what's her name? Ohlendorf—we ought to follow it up."

"Don't get yourself in an uproar. We'll see about it." Steve looked worried. "Do you think the old guy's telling the truth?"

"How should I know?"

"Well, let's get going."

"Please thank him for us," Andy said to the porter.

Old Joost followed them outside. The girl was nowhere in sight, but Andy heard the clanking of the cowbell behind the windmill.

As they approached the Citroën another car drove up from the direction of Oosterdijk. It was a white Volkswagen convertible with the word *Polizei* stenciled on the door. The Volkswagen came to a squealing stop and a policeman got out.

He said something sharply to the porter. Andy recognized the name Hilversum. The porter replied with his shrug. Old Joost said something, and the policeman wheeled on him with a question. Joost began to shout. Then he gasped, his knees buckled; and he fell heavily to the ground and lay there, face down, without moving. The policeman kneeled and began to chafe one of the big limp hands while the porter went into the house for some water. When he returned the policeman was no longer holding Old Joost's hand. He shook his head at the porter and spoke again in Dutch.

The porter said in English, "He is dead."

From Andy Longacre's diary:

. . . the second body. It had been in the ground much longer, for years. I get sick to my stomach even now, just thinking about it, because Steve and I hung around until the policeman, whose name is Vander Poel, finished digging it up.

In the second grave, Vander Poel found a passport. The identification photo had rotted away, but the cover was more or less intact. It was a British passport. Near the body—I don't know why, but this is the grisliest fact of all—Vander Poel found a rusted bicycle.

The serial number on that was intact and they traced it to the one bicycle shop in Oosterdijk. The proprietor had rented it, in 1948, to an English private investigator named Dickson.

All that was three days ago. Yesterday, the criminal-investigation team came down from Amsterdam and made its report. Vander Poel told me what the findings were, probably because he wants our co-operation. I'd better make the bicycle the second grisliest fact, because the autopsy showed that when Mrs. Hilversum was put into the ground she was still alive. The old man must have been off his rocker, at that.

I told Vander Poel all I knew, which isn't much—that we were looking for Milo Hacha because he's the heir to a large estate left by an American airman, whose life he'd saved in the war. At first Steve wouldn't give the testator's name, but Vander Poel got tough about it. He told us he would check all this with the American legation in Amsterdam. This made Steve very unhappy.

The girl Katrina has been sent to a foundling home in

Amsterdam. Vander Poel says she refuses to believe any-thing they say about her grandfather. Poor kid.

When they tell us we can leave Oosterdijk—after the in-quest or coroner's jury or whatever they have here—we're going to Lucerne, Switzerland, and look up Gertrude Ohlen-dorf.

The idea of going to Switzerland fascinates me, and I feel kind of guilty about that. It isn't merely Switzerland I want to see, either. It's Milo Hacha. There's a strange sort of magnetism even in the name for me now. I don't know what it is. All Oosterdijk remembers him as a hero of the re-sistance. Almost all Oosterdijk. Because Mayor Hilversum, for one, tried to build up a case against Hacha. Then there was Old Joost.

Did Joost kill twice to prevent anyone from finding Hacha's trail? If so, why? It doesn't make sense, because he quite eagerly told us Hacha wasn't dead. Why us?

There's talk, according to the porter, that Katrina Joost is really Milo Hacha's daughter. That figures. She sure looks Slavic enough. And the porter suggested, without coming out and naming any names, that I ought to be able to figure out who the mother was. He means Mrs. Hilversum, of course. Which could explain a thing or two.

She wanted Katrina to have Milo Hacha's legacy so she gave me the note? Then went out to see Old Joost—and got strangled for her trouble? Why? Because Old Joost didn't want it known that Hacha wasn't dead, and she found out somehow? But then why did he tell Steve and me?

And, since Vrouw Hilversum gave us the tip about Joost, why did she have to go out and see him herself? To make sure he told us what she wanted him to? That Katrina was Hacha's daughter?

One thing I'm not is a detective. But I've got this gnawing curiosity about Milo Hacha.

If only I could stop worrying about Steve. He seems ready to crack. He's really scared.

Maybe in Lucerne . . .

Part THREE

Interlude—Vierwaldstaettersee

————◆————

7

Now he looked like a musician entirely.

Watching him, Trudy Ohlendorf sighed. He was a robust man in his early forties. He wore a white linen suit with padded shoulders. He had glossy black hair graying picturesquely at the temples and the suggestion of a bald spot on the crown of his head.

The baton in his right hand looked very small and he waved it with great vigor. He was directing the Grand Orchestre du Casino in the garden of the Lucerne Kursaal Casino.

They were playing the Moldau music from Smetana's *My Fatherland*. He had explained the score to Trudy with enthusiasm, for he was a Sudeten German from Czechoslovakia, and loved his native music. It was program music, following the course of the Vltava River from its source in the dark Bohemian forest—rushing across the rock bed and through the black forestland, past hunters with their horns and peasants dancing to the roaring cataracts of the St. Johns Rapids and finally, majestically, wide and serene through Prague.

But it wearied Trudy. The magic had gone out of it simply because Heinz Kemba, musician, looked like a musician. This, Trudy knew, was unreasonable of her. But she had always catered to her whims and quirks. Why bother to be reasonable?

At first Heinz Kemba, musician, had looked to her like anything but a musician. When she had met him, almost a year before, on the Lucerne Lido she had taken him for a professional athlete. Professional athletes as such held no particular fascination for Trudy, but to discover him leading the orchestra with athletic vigor at the Kursaal . . . Their affair had lasted almost a year.

It was ending now. It was ending because the mystery was solved. There should be in a man an aura of the un-known, Trudy thought, to hold a woman, to challenge her.

Trudy had long suspected that she had allowed herself to have an affair with Heinz Kemka because he was an exiled Czech. . . . For that other exiled Czech had meant so much in her life. Milo Hacha. Just thinking his name made her breath come quickly. Milo Hacha. . . .

Good-by, Heinz, Trudy thought. Tonight, and then good-by. Of course good-by. The athlete was entirely gone and the complete musician stood there, coaxing the Moldau out of the Kursaal Orchestre in the garden on Haldenstrasse overlooking the dark, silent lake.

At the ringside table, listening to the music, Trudy Ohlen-dorf ordered another bottle of Pony Hell export beer. It was her third. When it came, the glass beaded with con-densed moisture, Trudy drank deeply. She was a handsome woman who was thirty-two and looked twenty-five. Her hair was chestnut, her legs long and pretty, although on the sturdy side. Swiss Alpine legs, Heinz Kemka had called them, caressing her with his big strong athlete-musician's hands. She wore a summer dress with a low neckline. It showed wide, smoothly curved shoulders, an expanse of flawless tanned skin and the beginning of a cleft between her breasts.

Tonight could be like any other night, Trudy Ohlendorf decided. Why not? She would tell Heinz that it was all over between them afterward. Perhaps she wouldn't even bother to explain. She was hoping he wouldn't make a scene. Already she had in mind exactly what she wanted to do.

A walk down Haldenstrasse to Schwanenplatz and over the old Chapel Bridge across the River Reuss (Moldau, she thought, and smiled) to the old quarter of town for some cheese fondue and a good white wine. A new Swiss wine, at the Wilden Mann, where the fondue was so thick a spoon would stand in it.

Then back across the bridge to Alpenstrasse, where Heinz had set her up in an apartment and where, tonight, they would make love for the last time. At dawn, a walk at the lakeside to watch the sun come up behind the snowy Alps. Heinz would express his amazement, for the three-hundredth morning, at her unflagging energy. At that moment he would look most like a musician and least like an athlete—his hair mussed, tired shadows under his eyes—and so then she would tell him.

The Vltava was now rushing stormily across the orchestra stage through the St. Johns Rapids, assisted by the elements. A real thunderstorm was in the air. The garden roof rolled shut overhead. Heinz softened the storm onstage with fluid movements of his big hands as he put the Vltava, in its wide and serene phase, through its paces in Prague.

Trudy finished her third Pony Hell and looked around. Now that the customers beyond the range of the sliding weather roof had scurried under it, the Kursaal garden was crowded. Trudy stared boldly at the men seated at the tables listening to the Vltava run its course.

They were so easy to figure out, most of them. Take that German burgher there. Obviously a businessman, his pockets stuffed with marks from the rebuilding of Köln or Koblenz or wherever.

Or that one. Dark and small and very French. Very suave, very sure of himself, very boring.

Or the young man talking anxiously to the maître d' and then making his way self-consciously across the garden. That one, surely, was an American student. He had no mystery, no surprises, absolutely none.

He was good-looking in a sapling sort of way. He had studied a guide-book on Lucerne and could name all the mountains in the vast rising ranges across the water. He would ascend Mt. Pilatus on the cograilway, spend a morning hiking along the cliff trails, stop for lunch and wine at Pilatus Kulm and go home saying he had climbed an Alp. . . .

Trudy yawned. And suddenly sat up straight. *That* was a surprise, at least. The American student seemed to be heading for her table. Now he had stopped, looking down at her. A slightly lopsided smile touched his mouth. He was actually going to speak to her.

"I beg your pardon," he said. "Miss Ohlendorf? Miss Gertrude Ohlendorf? Do you speak English? *Parlez-vous Français? Oder, sprechen Sie Deutsch?*"

"I can speak whichever you prefer," Trudy said in English.

"But I'm afraid you have an advantage over me."

"The name's Andrew Longacre. Most people call me Andy after one drink. May I buy you a drink?"

"Yes," Trudy heard herself answering. "Why, yes, Andy, I believe you can."

Andy sat down and signaled a waitress. The buxom Swiss girl obliged promptly. This surprised Trudy. Foreign students, she had noticed, were notoriously inept at summoning waiters or waitresses. Could she have been wrong about him?

He ordered two brandies. Neither of them spoke until the drinks had come, but the young American did not appear self-conscious now. He seemed quite composed.

"*Pros't*," he said, raising his drink.

"Cheers."

They drank.

"This probably won't take long," he said.

Trudy found herself thinking that that was regrettable. He was really not unattractive.

"Yes, Andy?" she smiled.

"I found you in the phone book and the concierge at your apartment building said you'd probably be here. The maître d' identified you for me." He grinned. "End of mystery."

End of mystery, nothing! Trudy thought. It was only the beginning.

Thunder boomed and crashed outdoors as the orchestra finished its Moldau. Heinz Kemka bowed, saw that Trudy was occupied, and went with a few of the musicians to a table reserved for them during intermissions.

Wasn't he even slightly annoyed that Trudy was with another man? He didn't look it. Now, after almost a year, he took her for granted. Well, if he wasn't annoyed, *she* was.

"What is it you want of me, Andy?" she asked softly.

"Like another drink?"

"Very much, I think."

He ordered two more brandies.

"I came here from Holland looking for you," he said.

"Then you are a detective?" He could have been a thousand things besides a detective, but the idea of a detective looking like a student fascinated her.

"No." He did not amplify.

"Well?"

"The people at CARE in The Hague told me you'd gone home to Lucerne."

"Then you are with CARE?"

"No, I'm not." Again he didn't amplify. Trudy sipped her brandy. He was young, very young. Twenty-one? Twenty-three? Young enough to be Heinz Kemka's son. But if he wasn't a detective, and wasn't with CARE, then who was he?

"In Oosterdijk, Holland, I was told a Czech named Milo Hacha was dead. Then—"

"Did you say Milo Hacha?" Trudy almost dropped her glass.

"Yes, that's right. Hacha."

"Go on. Please, go on." What could this boy have to do with Milo?

"Then we learned, my brother and I, that Hacha wasn't dead. We knew he was receiving CARE packages about ten years ago, and found out that you had tried to trace him for CARE. That's right, isn't it?"

"Yes."

"Have any luck?"

Trudy didn't answer immediately. She'd had luck, as he put it. Oh yes, she'd had luck. But Milo Hacha wasn't in Lucerne now.

She would never get over Milo Hacha. She automatically compared all the men in her life with Milo Hacha, and all suffered. That was inevitable, Hacha being Hacha. But if she told this interesting young American what she knew, he might go away.

"Well, yes and no," Trudy said.

Andy grinned ruefully. "That's a help."

Trudy found the look captivating. "But my dear Andy," she said, reaching across the little table and touching his hand, "assuming I *did* find Milo Hacha, and was supposed to report that fact and didn't—"

"Why didn't you?"

Trudy looked into his eyes. They were grayish-green and flecked with yellow. "Do you perhaps like cheese fondue?"

"To tell the truth, I've never tasted it."

"And do you perhaps like walking in the rain? Because I know where we can get the best cheese fondue in Switzerland."

Instead of answering, Andy beckoned the waitress. "Our

check, please. This is on me," he said. "We detectives have
expense accounts that would choke a horse."

Trudy squeezed his hand. He squeezed back. He made her
feel very young. While Andy paid the check she thought
of the walk in the rain, the Wilden Mann and afterward. . . .

Heinz Kemka mounted the podium and the first violinist
scratched out a tone for the other musicians. The lights in
the Kursaal garden dimmed and a flash of lightning across the
lake momentarily showed the brooding crag of Mt. Pilatus.

"And now," Trudy said, rising as he held her chair for
her, "no more talk of Milo Hacha for awhile. Fair enough?"

"It suits me fine," Andy said.

As they stepped out from under the protection of the
Kursaal garden's roof into the rain, Trudy noticed that Heinz
Kemka was watching them. Perhaps, this was the best way
of telling him good-by, after all.

The soft rain was like a caress.

8

The apartment had two rooms and was furnished in severe
Danish modern. "You like it?" Trudy asked.

"Very nice."

"I hate cluttered rooms."

Trudy seated herself on a sofa that resembled an open
sandwich, a slab of polished birch supporting a slab of foam
rubber. She spread her wide skirt out and smiled up at Andy.
"What are you thinking?"

Instead of answering, he smiled back. What he was thinking was that she was a beautiful woman and that he wanted
to make love to her, here, on this sandwich-of-a-sofa, immediately.

"What *are* you thinking?"

She really didn't want an answer. What he was thinking
was that a course ought to be given somewhere in the flirt-
ing mores of European women. How did you keep from
making a fool of yourself?

"Let's go to the Wilden Mann every night," she said. "Because the Kursaal was nothing. We really met there, at the Wilden Mann."

They had a great deal of fondue, Andy remembered, dipping it up with thick chunks of bread and washing it down with so much white wine that he had a pleasant buzz on. She had obviously enjoyed the cheese, the wine, his company, the walk in the rain. And most of all she had enjoyed his enjoyment of them. She had seemed pleased at their lack of conversation, as if she disliked people who talked too much. Then, coming here to her apartment on Alpenstrasse, when the rain had really pelted them, she had laughed like a child at the way he held her hand.

"I'm glad you don't want to tell me," she said.

"Tell you what?"

"What you're thinking, of course. There is brandy in the bar."

It was Martell V.S.O.P. He found two large, tinted snifters and poured a liberal shot in each. He watched her swirl the brandy and sip it. He did the same with his, standing over her. Suddenly she set the snifter on the floor and stretched like a cat. "Tired?"

He shook his head.

"You are not very talkative, either."

"I'm sorry," he said, watching her.

She laughed. "Who wants to talk?"

She swung her legs up on the slab of foam rubber and kicked off her shoes. She lay back, clasping her hands behind her head, watching him watch her breasts, her eyelids fluttering, closing. "Don't shut off the light."

Just before he kissed her on the mouth her eyes opened. They remained open as she flung her arms around his neck.

He carried her into the bedroom.

She was a big woman, but she felt weightless in his arms. He put her down on the bed. "Turn on the light," she said.

He turned the light on. She was undressing.

They made love and slept in each other's arms and made love again before Heinz Kemka's key turned in the lock of the apartment on Alpenstrasse.

Heinz Kemka was jealous.

He had never dreamed their affair would be permanent, of course. He knew Trudy's history too well for that. She had seemed compelled, over the months they were together, to tell him about her past lovers. It had amused him, until tonight.

Now he wondered what she would tell the earnest-looking boy about *him*. Trudy had often said that if you couldn't bare your heart to a lover, you should not bare your body.

One of her lovers had been a French existentialist poet who turned out to be a masochist. Another had been a retired British colonial officer who talked constantly about Clive and Kitchener. He made love as if he were fighting the Battle of Omdurman. A third had been a Spanish Republican exile who produced passionate motion pictures in Brussels, and conducted himself in bed as if he were directing one of them.

The fourth had been Milo Hacha.

Actually, Hacha had been the first. Trudy had been a virgin of twenty-one when she met him in the Netherlands while employed by CARE. Heinz Kemka, also a Czech, had heard of Hacha—or rather, of Hacha's father.

Rudolf Hacha had been a prominent Socialist politician in Czechoslovakia when the Nazis took over. A Democrat, he had been arrested but had managed to survive the concentration camp. Then, after the war, he had been one of the Social Democrats who refused to knuckle under to the Communists. The same morning that Masaryk's body was found in a courtyard Rudolf Hacha had been arrested again, and this time he was held in solitary confinement until the new government was ready to put him on trial for "treason" several months later.

Fearing for his life, Kemka assumed, the younger Hacha had remained in the Netherlands until he became involved in trouble of some sort. Then he had fled with Trudy.

There was a difference in Trudy's tone whenever she spoke of Milo Hacha. He was the only one she never made fun of. She had even admitted, in a weak moment, that while she had broken off with the other three, Hacha had broken with her.

Hacha, she said, had educated her. Hacha had exposed her to life and love. She even said she would have married him—had he asked her. He had been a riddle she could not solve.

Looking back, now, on the nights she had spoken of Hacha, Kemka realized that the seeds of his jealousy had already been planted. For Hacha, as Trudy remembered

Hacha, made Kemka feel less than a complete man. Still, on those nights her love-making was memorable.

And which part of the Hacha myth am I? Heinz Kemka had asked her more than once. But that is easy, Heinz, she would say, you are a Czech, he was a Czech. . . . It had not endeared Hacha to him.

At the conclusion of the program at the Kursaal, Heinz Kemka had taken a taxi to Zum Wilden Mann. The maître d'hôtel told him that Fräulein Ohlendorf had been in earlier. Kemka drank three double Scotches (it had been the British colonial officer's favorite drink, he even remembered that) and walked slowly back to Alpenstrasse.

It was his apartment. He paid the rent and he had furnished it. Was it possible Trudy would dare to entertain a new lover there?

He saw light in the living-room window. He went through the small lobby to the courtyard. There was light also in the bedroom window.

Heinz Kemka went upstairs.

He stood outside the door, breathing hard. There was no sound from the apartment.

He unlocked the door savagely. He slammed it so hard it made a sound like a rifle shot. He felt suddenly foolish.

The unknown young man, his face heavy with love, came out of the bedroom. He was wearing one of Kemka's robes. Trudy, also in a robe, one that Kemka had purchased for her birthday, was right behind him.

Heinz Kemka bellowed, lunged across the room and swung wildly at the young man.

------◆------

9

From Andy Longacre's diary:

. . . beginning to feel like a character in a Durrell novel.

It hardly seems we've already been in Lucerne a week. Seven days, and about the only time I've seen Steve is at breakfast. If he hadn't been too tired to go out that first night I met T— maybe all this would have worked out differently. Not that I'm complaining. Hell, I'm beginning to feel like a man of the world—whatever that means. A mistress and everything.

But who is keeping whom?

After that first gaudy night it settled down to merely (*merely!*) the seven most memorable days of my life. Not to mention (stop leering, Longacre) the nights.

I feel guilty about Steve, though. We had a sort of tacit understanding. As far as he knows, I'm busy trying to get information out of the difficult Miss O—. That suits Steve; looking for Milo Hacha has always been two steps forward and one back, as if he's not sure he wants to find the guy . . .

But Steve can't go on living in limbo like this, which is where my guilt feelings come in. I ought to be working at it day and night, and I'm not. Not at that, anyway. Steve, meanwhile, is trying to have himself a ball. He's really trying, but he's too gloomy.

We're staying at the Hotel Montana, so he generally walks down the hill after dinner to the Kursaal to try his luck at the boule tables. So far he hasn't dropped too much. Days, he just mopes around. Or so I gather. And at breakfast he hasn't mentioned Milo Hacha's name once.

If we ever do track down Hacha—and I'd be willing to bet now that we do—I wonder what Steve will do about it.

Lake Lucerne—which the natives call the Lake of the Four Cantons, or Vierwaldstaettersee—is one hell of a fine spot for a vacation. It's deep and blue and clear, and all the municipal piers and mooring posts are whitewashed a dazzling white. And there are plump white swans in the water. The city is on the west shore of the lake, a labyrinth of crooked medieval streets and cobbled squares with ornate fountains gushing icy mountain water at almost every corner.

To the east are the lower Alps, green and rounded, with the Rigi dominating them. To the south, seen distantly across the blue water and on clear days rearing impossibly high into the blue sky, are the higher snowy Alps.

They inspire awe, sure; but there's something serene and comforting about them, too. I tried to put it into words for T— once, but she only laughed and said her "detective" was a frustrated poet. That night she was really something in bed, but I guess there's no connection.

T—'s a big, lusty girl with a tremendous appetite for life. Girl—she's probably ten years older than I am. She says, quite matter-of-factly, that love is her one talent.

She means physical love, and we both let it go at that. Because only once in her life was there any other kind of love to go along with it, and that one time was Milo Hacha.

The other night after dinner I asked her if she had a picture of Hacha. She smiled a little sadly and shook her head. Then she said, "You do not understand about Milo Hacha. He destroys his past. How do you say it?—he burns his bridges. I had a photograph, yes. But I no longer have it. His lives are separate. A life for the Netherlands, a life for here, a life for—where he's gone."

"Where did he go?"

"But if I tell you, you'll go away, too."

"I came here looking for Hacha," I admitted.

"And found me." She took my hand, and kissed the palm and placed it on her breast, so of course we stopped talking about Milo Hacha.

It's been like that ever since the first night. That first night was something out of a comic opera. We were asleep in bed when I heard a bang. I'm a slow waker. T— was slipping into her robe while I was still knuckling the sleep out of my eyes.

"You look just like a little boy, Andy."

I mumbled something.

"It's Heinz." She padded to the closet and brought me a robe. "Here."

"Heinz?" That woke me fast. "Don't tell me you're married!"

She shook her head. "Silly."

I put the robe on and she prodded me ahead of her out into the living room. I began to feel like fifty-seven varieties of damn fool.

I recognized him right away. He was the orchestra leader at the Kursaal garden.

He opened his mouth and made a loud noise, then charged.

He swung, wrapping his arm around my neck. I shoved him away. His fist bounced off my shoulder. So I swung—and missed. It was like one of those quickie movie fights, very badly directed. We moved around each other like a couple of hams in a vaudeville show.

I pushed with both hands flat against his chest and gave T—

a despairing look. She seemed amused. But looking at her was a mistake. He hit me in the stomach and I doubled over.

When I straightened up, my head butted his face. Right away his nose started to bleed. He snuffled, but the blood ran like a faucet.

"It's his poor nose!" T—cried. She took him by the arm and led him, unresisting, to the sofa. He stretched out on his back with his head dangling over the edge. "Quick," T— told me. "Get a wet towel." Would you believe it? I ran for one.

She frowned at me when I got back. "No, no! Wring it out."

So I went back to the bathroom and wrung out the towel. When I brought it back, Kemka snatched it from me, glaring. They seemed to know just what to do. So after a while I went into the bedroom and got dressed.

When I returned, the bleeding had stopped and T— was patting Kemka's hand. "I'll be out of here in the morning," she said in German.

Kemka must have felt ridiculous. I know I sure did.

"Are you all right?" I asked.

"*Ja, ja,*" he said. "It is nothing. The nose bleeds easily, that's all."

"Well, can I get you a cab?"

My fatuous solicitude practically made him speechless. All he could say was "I live here." He had me there. I picked up my hat.

T— walked me into the hall. "I'll call you in the morning," she said. "Where are you staying?"

"The Montana. Is it—I mean, will you be—?"

"When his nose bleeds like that he moves around for at least a day as if he is made from china."

When I kissed her she began to giggle. "His eyes," she whispered. "Did you see his eyes? He was furious."

She pushed me gently from Kemka's apartment.

———————◆———————

10

"No, listen, Ron," Estelle Street said into the telephone. "He was from the legal affairs section of the State Department."

"I still say you're making a mountain out of a molehill," Ronald Hurley told her.

"But Barney's will hasn't been probated yet, has it?"

"I'm your lawyer, Estelle. Let me handle this."

"Has it?"

"Well, no."

"The State Department lawyer knew the name of the beneficiary. I'm worried, Ron. I'm scared sick. I don't want to lose that money, do you hear me? I don't want to lose it."

"Well, you can stop your worrying. I said I'd handle it."

"But what if Milo Hacha's alive?"

"I don't care if he's alive and has fourteen starving kids," Hurley said. "I can conduct the best investigation on paper you ever saw." He laughed. "And I've got friends when the time comes for probation. So will you just calm down?"

"How can I calm down? Steve Longacre found out that Hacha was still alive. He wrote me from Holland."

"From Holland? What the hell are you talking about?"

Estelle told him. Then she said, "Don't you see, Ron? If you do it your way, even if you're successful, I'll spend the rest of my life expecting him to turn up."

"You idiot! It was Steve's poking around that got the State Department interested. If you had to send someone, why'd you pick that damn has-been?"

"Don't talk to me like that," Estelle said. "And that's one of the reasons I called you. Ron, tell me who did the job on Barney."

"I can't hear a word you say."

"I don't trust Longacre any more. I realize he was a mistake, but at the time he was all I had."

"I'm glad you feel that way. Call him off, Estelle. Fast."

"Who did the job on Barney?"

"Listen—"

"No. You listen to me. I was clearing out some of Barney's stuff. I found something." Estelle paused, but Hurley remained silent. "Steve Longacre isn't the only one I can send to the chair now."

"What did you find, Estelle?"

"Take three guesses, and the first two don't count."

"Damn you, stop playing games with me!"

"There's another copy of Barney's deposition. I have it.

In a safe place. With the usual instructions if anything happens to me."

". . . Estelle?"

"I'm still here."

"What do you want?" Hurley's crisp voice sounded tired and defeated.

"I had a photostat made. Would you like to see it?"

"I asked you, what do you want?"

"Two million dollars, Ron. Minus lawyer's fees."

"So?"

"The only way I can call off Longacre is in person, because I don't know where he is now. I'll have to track him down. I intend to do that. But I still intend to do the rest of it my way. Tell me, Ron, if the heir's dead . . ."

"You get the estate as Barney's next of kin. We went all through that."

"Who did the job on Barney?"

"Estelle—"

"Because I have another job for them, Ron. Well?"

Hurley sighed and said, "All right, I'll set up a meeting for you. But I still think you're making a mistake."

"When?"

"After you show me the photostat."

"I love you, too, Ron. . . ."

Estelle smiled and hung up.

Steve Longacre awoke in the night, sweating from a dream.

He went into the bathroom and sloshed cold water on his face. He was trembling. He had had the same dream before. His face in the mirror over the sink looked old. There were purplish pouches under his eyes.

In the dream he had killed the man exactly as he had killed him in real life. Except that the details were clearer. . . .

It had been raining. A cold, steady rain, drumming on the black asphalt just before midnight. Cars sped by, their headlights sending yellow probing shafts ahead, tires whispering on the wet streets.

Steve had stood waiting in the rain with a man named Chester Little. Chicken Little, they called him. Chicken was a nerveless little man with a high, happy voice and absolutely no regard for human life. Chicken, in Sing Sing now, wouldn't have that dream. Murder was his business. It was something you did to earn a buck. . . .

What's the matter with that kid, Steve thought. We've got to find this Hacha. He rubbed a damp palm across his forehead and groaned. Sometimes he didn't want to find Hacha at all. Sometimes he thought he would rather die than find him. He had killed a man only once. He did not think he could do it again.

In the dream, as in real life, the door had opened just before midnight. It was the front door of a white clapboard house on Front Street, just outside the business district in Hempstead. A man stood silhouetted in the doorway with light behind him.

"That the bum?" Chicken Little had asked in his shrill voice.

They stood on the dark sidewalk, in the rain, thirty yards from the yellow rectangle. A girl appeared beside the man. She held his arm and smiled up at him.

They spoke, but Steve couldn't hear the words. Then the girl stood on tiptoes and kissed the man on the lips. He came down the flagstone walk, moving briskly, and she waved and shut the door. The man passed by the light that stood on a post at the beginning of the flagstone walk. Steve had seen his face very clearly. The man's name was Joey Imparato and he had been fingered for Steve in Nino's Restaurant in Westbury after the trotters at Roosevelt Raceway.

Joey Imparato ran a small garbage-trucking firm in two Oyster Bay towns in the days before garbage collection had gone municipal. He had been asked politely to amalgamate with the big boys. He had refused just as politely. He had been asked again, not so politely. He had refused not so politely. One of his haulers was mauled after leaving the dump in Syosset. Then Joey had made a lot of noise about organizing the half-dozen or so independent garbage firms that were left and along with the noise went unexpected progress. So the word was passed: Joey Imparato had to be hit.

"That the bum?" Chicken Little repeated.

Steve's throat had felt funny; he could only nod. Chicken smiled expectantly. They had been standing in the cold rain for almost three-quarters of an hour waiting for Joey

Imparato to come out after walking his girl friend home from the movies.

"He must of laid the broad," Chicken had said. "He'll die happy."

Chicken Little had fired, twice. Joey Imparato spun around and started to fall. In the dream there was a surprised look on Joey's face, but that couldn't have been, for by then he was out on the sidewalk and they wouldn't have been able to see his face in the dark.

Steve had fired, too. His hand was shaking, so he probably missed, but that didn't matter. He was just as guilty as Chicken.

After Steve fired, Chicken had run over, stood over Joey, and shot him point-blank four times more. Then the revolver clicked on an empty chamber.

Things had happened fast after that. The front door of the clapboard house opened and the girl started to yell. A car, the getaway car, roared up the block and came to a stop.

The car had been stolen in Hicksville and Lou Goody, who could make your hair stand on end with the tricks he could pull behind a wheel, was driving.

But another car was behind him. It was a blue-and-orange county patrol car. The siren started its scream. Steve ran to the car Lou Goody was driving. Chicken Little, running across the wet street, wasn't so lucky. He slipped on the slick asphalt and fell down in the path of the police car.

"Close the freakin' door!" Lou Goody shouted.

Steve had slammed it and they shot away from the curb.

By the time one of the cops could jump out and collar Chicken, Lou had had a fair head start. They careened out of Hempstead and along the Bethpage Turnpike. They could hear the siren wailing behind them.

Goody swung the car, tires screeching, north on Post Avenue. This made very good sense, for the crowds from the old Roosevelt Raceway, slowed by the rain, were still funneling out of the raceway exit. But then, Lou Goody was a very good getaway man.

They joined the raceway traffic heading north. The cop lost them there. They abandoned the stolen car in Westbury and went into Felice's Restaurant, where Lou Goody ordered a seafood supper for both of them. The sight and the smell of the food made Steve sick. He rushed to the men's room and vomited.

Later, Goody phoned a friend who drove them home to Mineola, where they spent the night at Lou's apartment.

That was where the dream ended, but there was more than the dream involved.

Two days later Steve was arrested and booked on suspicion of murder. The grand jury was unable to present a prima-facie case against him, and he was released. The fact that Chicken Little—who drew a life sentence—implicated him didn't matter legally.

Section 399 of the Criminal Code of the State of New York states: "A conviction cannot be had upon the testimony of an accomplice, unless he is corroborated by such other evidence as tends to connect the defendant with the commission of the crime."

The boys who were left in the garbage-hauling business paid Barney Street his price. Joey Imparato's two towns were taken over. They were well satisfied.

But a week before Joey Imparato died with six bullets from Chicken Little's revolver in his body, Estelle Street had overheard a conversation between her husband and her one-time lover. While she was quietly making herself a drink in the living room, she had heard it all from the adjoining dining room.

Estelle knew she shouldn't have overheard that conversation, so she put her coat on, slammed the door and came in a second time with a loud, cheerful greeting.

Estelle waited six months before she told Steve. Now, in Lucerne, with the dream bringing it all back, Steve broke out in a cold sweat as he paced the floor.

Would he kill Milo Hacha? Could he?

The door opened and Andy came in. His face was flushed; he looked happy. He had been sobered by the events in Holland, but most of the time Andy had seemed to regard their European trip as a jaunt. That was all right with Steve. All Andy knew was that they had to find a man named Hacha because of Barney Street's will. As for the real purpose of the trip, to kill Hacha if he was alive . . .

"What are you doing up?" Andy asked.

"One of those nights. I couldn't sleep. How'd it go, kid?"

"How'd what go?"

"You know, with the Ohlendorf broad. You saw her, didn't you?"

"Yes," Andy said. "I saw her."

"Well, is she going to talk or isn't she? Does she know where Hacha went?" Steve licked his dry lips. "We been in Lucerne eight days now. You like it here? You want to settle down or something?"

"Hey, take it easy."

"I didn't mean to yell at you."

"Okay."

"Don't tell me," Steve said suddenly, "you've made time with her already."

"Did I say that?" Andy tried not to sound belligerent.

"You look it. What is it, love? What are you so close-mouthed about, Andy?"

"Let's say there are some things I don't like to kick around," Andy said shortly. "Even with my brother. Now how about hitting it, Steve? We're both bushed."

"You know when I get like this I can't sleep," Steve said. "Anyway, this works out great. You oughtn't to have any trouble pumping the broad now."

"She's not a broad!" Andy heard himself yelling.

"Okay, okay."

Andy sat down on the edge of his bed and began to undress. "Steve. Suppose I find out about Milo Hacha—say, tomorrow. What's on the program when I do?"

Andy looked up. Steve had turned away and gone over to the window, staring out as if the street lights on Haldenstrasse, the absolute blackness of the lake, the thrusting bulk of the mountains beyond against the lightening sky were irresistibly attractive.

Andy felt a sudden chill. He began to say more. But then he swallowed the question.

"I'm turning in, Steve. Good night."

"Good night, kid," Steve said.

Andy saw him shiver.

Part FOUR

Mueller

◆

11

Europe lay gasping under the hottest summer in years.

The heavy rains fell early that year, and the heat followed them. From Cape Passero in Sicily to the German Baltic ports, from Brest to the Elbe River, the Continent lay smothering.

The great cross-country busses, an institution in German-speaking countries, a week before had been floundering and slipping hub-deep in mud on the secondary roads. Now they were leaving clouds of thick, yellow dust from Schleswig to Carinthia. Their gleaming glass roofs parboiled the American tourists who staggered out to view the ruins of the *Schloss* at Heidelberg and the baroque splendor of the brand-new, rebuilt State Opera House on The Ring in Vienna.

Gerhard Mueller was waiting at the Goldener Hirsch in Salzburg, Austria, for the bus he was to drive. He was a short, flabby man sweating through the gray Tyrolean jacket that was his uniform. The driver who had brought the bus through the Tyrol from Innsbruck gave Mueller a limp greeting and repaired to the Goldener Hirsch for a cool drink.

Mueller waited until the tourists took their pictures of the Horse Mural, and then they piled back into the big Mercedes-Benz for more punishment. He held his right hand out and looked at it. The fingers were still trembling. The day before, he had almost been killed.

Mueller entered the bus and sat down, his heavy, damp

thighs filling the driver's bucket seat. He swiveled his beefy neck once to look at his tourist passengers.

There was the usual assortment of old maids, school-teachers with guidebooks, harassed couples with teen-aged children. All were Americans. The passenger representative, in his natty uniform, was explaining in English why on this particular express tour they could not stop over in Salzburg but must drive straight through, beyond Linz, to Vienna.

It had not been many kilometers from Linz where, yesterday, Gerhard Mueller had almost been killed.

For a thousand schillings, he thought. Nobody had told him he'd be shot at, and he hadn't even collected his money yet. He was to get it in Vienna from Dieter Loringhoven, who had a room in the Hotel Astoria on the Kärntnerstrasse. Loringhoven would be pleased. He would get the money. But never again!

Just as Gerhard Mueller was about to pull out of the broad square between the Goldener Hirsch and the Horse Mural, someone banged on the outside of the door. Mueller pulled the lever and the door opened.

Two men stood there in the dust of the square. They wore suits with the unmistakable sheen of American wash-and-wear fabric. One looked about forty and the other not much more than half that age. The passenger representative, whose name Mueller did not yet know because he was new, the replacement for Milo Hacha, hurried over and smiled dutifully down at the Americans.

In German the younger American asked, "Is Gerhard Mueller aboard? In Innsbruck they said Mueller would be with this bus."

"I am Mueller," Mueller said. The younger man nodded. The older one looked unhappy, but relieved.

The passenger representative wrote out two tickets, took their traveler's check and gave them a few schillings in change. They climbed into the bus, found two vacant seats and sat down.

Gerhard Mueller slipped the big Mercedes-Benz into first and drove off, leaving a dust cloud in the square.

There had been dust yesterday too, on the border above Linz and Freistadt and more dust, choking yellow swirls of it, on the secondary road which ran north into Czechoslovakia, between the Vltava River and the main highway from Ceske Budejovice through the Tábor in Prague.

To earn his thousand schillings Mueller had taken Milo Hacha only as far as Ceske Budejovice. He needed the money; what with a wife and two children in Innsbruck and a mistress in Vienna, a bountiful blonde who liked the pastries at Demel's and the expensive dinners at the Sacher Hotel. So Mueller had agreed to guide Milo Hacha across the border at Dieter Loringhoven's proposal.

Hacha, an exile like himself, was going in secrecy to Prague to face a great future, it seemed. At first Hacha had undoubtedly been suspicious. It must have taken all Dieter Loringhoven's eloquence to persuade him; Hacha was nothing if not canny. Wasn't the Czech regime widening, like Gomulka's Polish Communist Party, to include other Socialist elements? And hadn't Milo Hacha's father been a hero of the people?

In the end, Hacha had agreed, and Mueller had been selected to take him across the border, not only because they knew each other, but because Mueller knew the border from his activities in the black market during the occupation.

But why the secrecy? Why had Milo Hacha to sneak like a fugitive across the border? And why, most importantly from Gerhard Mueller's point of view, since it had almost cost him his life, hadn't his friend Siroky been at the Czech border station to pass him through again on his way back? But Siroky, who had regularly taken ten percent of Mueller's profits during the black-market days, was gone, and Mueller had never seen any of the other border guards before.

He had asked for Siroky. In reply, they had demanded his papers. Since he had no papers, he made a dash for it. They had chased him back away from the border. They shouted for him to stop and he ignored them, so they shot at him. He ran until he fell.

Then he had hidden in a hayfield, listening to the big crows overhead, to the distant train whistle, to his own heart banging against his ribs and finally to the jack boots of the border guards tramping through the hay.

All night Gerhard Mueller had remained in that hayfield. His body was trembling and he could not stop sweating. He had expected to die at any moment. It was the longest night of his life.

When it grew light enough to see his hand as a white blur he had made his way stealthily across the field, heading east. Here the Vltava River was little more than a stream, and he was able to wade across. A dog barking somewhere had made him flounder from the swift, knee-deep water, water as cold as acid, and begin to run.

He had gone east two kilometers, before the sun came up. In the distance he saw the pine-covered hills of the Bohemian forest. Soon he had heard some belled cows and seen a little yellow cottage nestling at the foot of the first slope; it had half-timbering on the walls and a steep gable roof. At the front door a heavy-chested horse waited patiently in the traces of a wagon.

Mueller remembered staring at the wagon, afraid and yet tempted. Then the distant dog had barked again, and it had sent him sprinting toward the wagon.

At that moment a gaunt, hard-faced man in farm clothing had stepped out of the house. Mueller, ready to take to his heels, had stammered a greeting in Czech and said he was heading for Ceske Krumlov, a small rural village near the border.

"I am going to Ceske Krumlov," the farmer said in a rusty voice, and Gerhard Mueller had clambered into the wagon with a silent prayer of thankfulness.

The road southward was narrow and unpaved. The wagon jolted and clanked. The farmer never spoke another word. Mueller recalled dozing, and in his doze dreaming that he was back in Vienna, window-shopping along The Graben for a thousand-schilling present for his buxom mistress. It was from this pleasant reverie that the farmer's nudge roused him, and he had opened his eyes to find himself at the shabby little free market of the village.

The farmer had not even answered his wave.

He had walked quickly south. When he saw the border station he tasted fear again and left the road. It was still early morning. No more than ten hours had passed since he had left Milo Hacha. He was hungry and tired. He had climbed a little hill and looked down on Austria.

Ten or twelve meters below, a border guard in an olive-colored uniform stood staring in the same direction. Then Gerhard Mueller had picked up a rock, made his way down the slope like an animal, crept up behind the guard and swung. The man had dropped without a sound.

And he . . . he had to run for his life.

Now, driving the big bus through Gmunden on the road to Linz, where there would be a stop for dinner, for the first time Mueller could dwell logically on what had happened.

What had happened was that they had tried to kill him. For crossing the border illegally? Of all the satellite countries, Czechoslovakia was the most prosperous—the West Germany of the Soviet camp—with little to fear from contamination by the West.

Then why had they tried to kill him?

At first he thought Dieter Loringhoven might be able to tell him, but as the bus neared Linz Mueller wasn't so sure. The more he thought about it, the less he liked the idea of asking Loringhoven. And by the time he had driven across the Danube bridge and into Linz along the Volksgartenstrasse, his panic had grown to include Dieter Loringhoven.

Hacha's return to Czechoslovakia was a secret, that had been impressed upon him by Loringhoven. But he, Mueller, shared the secret. Then was it no coincidence that they had tried to kill him? Had Loringhoven perhaps planned it that way? Was Loringhoven as ruthless as he was suave?

Gerhard Mueller groaned. One thousand schillings. One thousand schillings would make Theresa very happy.

He parked the Mercedes-Benz under the chestnut trees on the Volksgartenstrasse. As the tourists filed out, the passenger representative was recommending roast pork with *Knödel* and, of course, *Linzer torte*. Three or four of the passengers stopped to snap pictures. But the two Americans who had asked for him when they boarded the bus seemed to be waiting to speak to him. What could it be about?

———◆———

12

From Andy Longacre's diary:

. . . in bed together one final time.

T——knew what I wanted, of course. I'd asked her about Milo Hacha three days running. Probably the weather had something to do with her attitude. Lucerne, like any vacation spot, can be pretty dismal in the rain. It rained on and off for two days, with a low, dark sky hanging over the lake when it wasn't raining, hiding the mountains. Then the third day dawned bright and hot as hell. I asked her that day, too, but she remained peevish. Then, all of a sudden on the fourth night, after I promised Steve I'd get him an answer, she told me.

The funny part of it was, I didn't even ask her that night. We'd made love in T——'s room at the Wilden Mann, but it was still pretty early so we got out of bed, had some drinks and got into a discussion about, of all things, Comparative Lit.

T——likes Schiller and Goethe. The discussion got a little involved and I started giving her my theories as to why Switzerland had never produced any notable poets. After a while I was doing all the talking.

T——listened with a pretty pout on her face. I thought it was because I'd run down her native country, but then she said, unexpectedly, "Yes, Andy, I see you're a student after all."

I didn't say anything. She seemed disappointed about something, and went on, "Milo Hacha is in Austria. He's a passenger representative for Cosmic Tours on their Innsbruck-Vienna line. At least he was the last time he sent me a post card—about six months ago. And now I suppose you will be leaving?"

Since something had started her talking about Hacha, I didn't want her to stop. "What kind of guy is he?" I asked.

A world of longing came into her voice. "No kind of guy, Andy. Or perhaps every kind of guy there is. I suppose, basically, he's an opportunist."

"Guiding a bunch of tourists through Austria?"

She shrugged. "He has his reasons. Or perhaps it's a hiatus in his life. You'll know when you find him. You *are* going after him?"

"Yes."

She filled her glass and mine. We were drinking the new Swiss white wine she liked so much. "And after tonight I won't see you again?"

"It can keep one more day," I said. "How about going up to Pilatus in the morning?"

She smiled and touched my cheek with her hand. "So you are a sentimentalist," she said. "I think I like that. I'd like to believe you'll never forget me. But a year from now you probably won't even remember my name."

"I'll never forget you," I said. I wasn't trying to be gallant. I meant it.

We kissed and had another glass of the Swiss wine, then I left.

The next morning, when I called for her at the Wilden Mann, T—— had already checked out. She left no forwarding address, but there was a letter for me. I sat down in Zum Wilden Mann and ordered a glass of white wine and read what she had written:

Darling,

I hate good-bys, I want to remember you as you were last night. I hope you aren't too disappointed.

As I told you, Milo Hacha is an opportunist. He is also a very clever gambler. Here in Lucerne he lived for two years, supporting me in style, on his steady but unspectacular wins at the Kursaal boule tables. And, should the occasion arise, I believe he could be quite ruthless. I want you to be careful.

Please believe these are not the words of a jilted lover, though it's true—excluding yourself—that of the men I've loved, only Milo Hacha left me.

About our literature—or lack of it: We Swiss are too busy enjoying the good things in life to produce masterpieces. The same is true of Austria, which you are about to visit. Masterpieces are not produced, my student, from love of life. They are produced from despair.

Auf Wiedersehen,

T——

Twenty-four hours later Steve and I were on our way by train to Innsbruck. Steve hardly opened his mouth the whole trip. What's behind all this? Whatever it is, Steve is plenty worried. About me, maybe? I'm pretty sure he regrets having let me talk him into taking me along.

The Cosmic Tours office in Innsbruck is located on Maria Theresienstrasse. In German I asked a man there named Kuhn about Milo Hacha. Herr Kuhn was willing but confused.

He threw his hands up in mock anguish, then settled his heavy Tyrolean rump comfortably on his chair. "Men like Milo Hacha I will never understand. He was the best passenger representative we ever had. We were considering him for an executive job either here or in our main office in Vienna—and what does he do?"

He mopped the sweat from his face and went on, "I will tell you what he does. He quits. Like that. With no warning. A week ago he said he was through. This being the height of the tourist season, we were, of course, shorthanded. But does that disturb Herr Hacha? No, certainly not. I tell you—"

"Then he isn't with Cosmic Tours any more?"

"He is—poof!" Herr Kuhn said expressively. "Vanished into thin air. That is Shakespeare. Did you know?"

"There's no way we could trace him?"

Herr Kuhn thought about that for a moment. "Well, there is always Mueller," he said at last. "Mueller, you see, generally drove Milo Hacha's bus. On the road they roomed together. If anyone knows where Hacha went, Gerhard Mueller is the man."

I translated for Steve, and Steve said through his teeth, "Ask him where Mueller is now."

I asked him. He opened a green-covered book and ran a finger like a sausage down a list written in pencil. "Mueller has now four days off. He is to meet our bus at eleven tomorrow in Salzburg."

"*Danke,* Herr Kuhn."

We decided to take the night train to Salzburg, which got us there a little before one the next morning. We took a room at the Goldener Hirsch Hotel and slept like a couple of cadavers.

The bus was already there when we came out onto the Siegmunds Platz in front of the hotel. A few minutes later we were on our way to Vienna, via Linz, with Gerhard Mueller at the wheel.

When we reached Linz, where there was a stop for dinner, I approached Gerhard Mueller, smiled and asked in excellent German, "My brother and I were wondering if we could have dinner with you, Herr Mueller."

"Yes, of course," Mueller said.

"Good. We'd like to ask you some questions."

"But surely the passenger representative—"

"Questions about a friend of yours," I said. "Milo Hacha."

I gave him the usual story about looking for Milo Hacha in connection with a legacy of unspecified size. He cut me off hastily. "But Milo Hacha is no longer in Austria."

"Then where is he?"

"He is gone," said Gerhard Mueller. The soup came and he ate it noisily. It was a clear broth with liver dumplings in it.

"Gone where?"

He shrugged.

"When did you see him last?"

Mueller pretended to give it some thought. He was one of the worst liars I have ever encountered. "Last week," he said finally. "When we worked together on this bus."

"How much?" I asked Steve in English.

"A C-note ought to buy his grandmother," Steve grunted.

"I have a hundred dollars for you," I said to Mueller, "if you can remember where Hacha went."

If Steve expected him to fall on his face in the direction of Mecca, he had another expectation coming. Mueller didn't bat an eye.

"Why do you wish to find him?"

"I already told you. Well?"

He leaned across the table toward me. He had rotten teeth and a breath that was equally bad. "Did Dieter Loringhoven send you?" he asked in a hoarse whisper.

"I never heard of anyone named Loringhoven. All we want is to find Milo Hacha."

He picked a fish bone from his teeth. He was having a rough time making up his mind. "Let me see your passports, please."

He turned to the blank visa pages and studied the stamp, dated yesterday, which had been made at the Swiss-Austrian frontier. When he handed our passports back, his eyes were shiny slits in their folds of fat. "You will not wish to follow Milo Hacha where he went."

"Let us decide that."

"*Bitte.* The money."

I gave him fifty dollars. "Milo Hacha has gone to Czechoslovakia," he said, and stopped. Then he continued, "That is on account."

He held out his plump hand. I counted out the balance in Austrian schillings, which we'd obtained for traveler's checks at the Goldener Hirsch. Herr Mueller was an expert at making money disappear.

"All right, produce. How soon is he coming back?"

"But you don't understand," Mueller grinned. "He is never coming back. He has been offered an important post with the Czech government."

I turned to Steve and translated. "I guess that busts it—unless you want to hang around in Vienna for a couple of weeks trying to wrangle a Czech visa. But it would be a waste of time, Steve. They'd never let us in."

"I got to get hold of him," Steve mumbled. "You think this chiseler is telling the truth?"

"Now I do."

"All right. Let me think. Let me think about it."

We all piled back into the bus for the long ride to Vienna. We entered the old Austrian capital just before midnight and drove along the Mariahilferstrasse to the broad Opern Ring and along that to Karl Lueger Ring and from there to the Regina Hotel on Roosevelt Platz. I must admit I got a bang out of the stately avenues and baroque public buildings with their fantastic spotlighted statuary. I'm going to like Vienna.

Steve's decided to stay, at least for the present. He's crazy, though, if he thinks we can get Czech visas and poke around behind the Iron Curtain.

I'm writing this in our room at the Regina, waiting for Steve. Last I saw of him was in the lobby after we'd checked in. He was just leaving with Herr Mueller. Since Mueller's English is just about nonexistent, and Steve doesn't speak German, apparently they're going to find a translator of their own. Which means Steve doesn't want me in on whatever he's planning.

I hope to hell he knows what he's doing.

I have one of those feelings that won't float. It tells me we're getting into something deep. Why won't Steve loosen up?

13

The lights were on late in the little apartment in the huge, gray-stone apartment building on the Praterstrasse. Although most of the imperial city had been rebuilt since the war, this area, the old Russian zone of occupation, was still shabby with neglect.

Once the apartment had been expensive and chic, and from its windows you could look down four stories onto the Prater, with its grass and trees and fairyland lights. But now the view was weedy and disreputable. As soon as the Russians had gone and relocation began, the Prater had passed swiftly from upper to middle to lower class. In a few years, it would be a slum.

In the bedroom of the apartment where the lights burned at three A.M., Gerhard Mueller was undressing, a fleshy narrow-shouldered penguin of a man in rumpled underwear. "Well, what do you think?" he chuckled. "What do you think of your Gerhard now?"

The woman waiting for him in the bed made an uncomplimentary noise, the Viennese equivalent of a Bronx cheer. She wore a slightly frayed, very old but very well-cared-for black-silk nightgown. Because of the heat, which smothered the city even at this hour, she had not drawn the sheet over her body.

She was a large woman with full breasts threatening the old black silk, broad, peasant hips, but long and surprisingly slim legs. Her face was red with coarse pores, but she had thick blond hair, which she kept retinting the most fashionable shade.

"Well, what do you think?" Gerhard Mueller repeated.

"I haven't seen the American's money."

"I know, but—"

"And Dieter Loringhoven has a thousand schillings waiting for you. Are you dotty, Gerhard?"

"Five hundred dollars, that's what the American said. You heard. You translated, Theresa."

"You have already earned Dieter Loringhoven's money. Go and get it."

"I'm afraid of him."

67

"But not afraid of crossing the border again with the American? What's the matter with you?"

"Siroky wasn't at the border station. Maybe Loringhoven arranged that. Maybe I was supposed to be killed. Do you think I dare face Loringhoven after that?"

Theresa yawned. "Go to bed then. We'll talk about it in the morning."

Mueller looked at the woman. His mistress. Desire surged through him suddenly. "I'm not tired," he said. "Are you?" He went over and sat down beside her.

"Listen to me, Gerhard," she said, drawing up her legs lazily. "You're no bargain. Do you think I let you sleep with me because you're irresistible? I'll have nothing to do with you—nothing, you hear?—until you get the money from Loringhoven."

"Theresa."

"Take your stupid hands off me."

"*Liebchen. Bitte, bitte.*"

But she pushed his hand away contemptuously. "I said no, Gerhard. Go sleep in the other bed."

"Theresa—!"

"To the other bed, little man."

Gerhard Mueller straightened slowly. He felt an obscure, devouring grievance. He had almost been killed recrossing the border, he was afraid to see Loringhoven, and with the sour-faced American he was still up in the air. And now Theresa . . . He hurled himself upon her.

She rolled swiftly over and he fell face down upon the bed with an *oomph!* that made her laugh. She laughed and laughed, her breasts shaking like jelly.

Mueller got to his knees. He was quite pale. "*Schufte,*" he said. "*Hündin. Hure.*"

Theresa struck him in the face. What right did he have calling her a whore! The blow dazed him. His ears rang; he tasted blood. With a murderous cry he grabbed for her, trying to hurt her—for his brush with death at the border, for his fear of Loringhoven, for his indecision about the American, for the delectable flesh she was denying him.

Theresa's eyes widened. She began to struggle. The blood from his nose stained her hair, the sheet, the pillowcase. Their breaths labored and mingled on the squeaking bed.

She was powerful, and fifteen years his junior. Slowly she forced Mueller back, pinning him down, lying on him with her immovable weight. He writhed helplessly beneath her, crushed, humiliated, weeping for his inadequate manhood.

"Will you get the money from Loringhoven?" she panted in his ear. She ground him deeper into the bed. "Will you?" Deeper. *"Will you . . . ?"*

Then a remarkable thing happened. Through the pain in his body, through the tears of self-pity in his eyes, Gerhard Mueller became aware of the fury and contempt draining rapidly from the face above him. With wonder he saw her lips go slack, part, show the tip of her tongue; he saw her eyes half-close in a sort of agony and then distend in naked animal expectancy. To his astonishment the weight upon him vanished, Theresa vanished. He heard vaguely a ripping sound, as of a garment being torn away. Then she was upon him once more, with her lips, her hands, with everything.

It was the best night Mueller had ever had with her. It made him feel like a young lion.

He fell asleep as if she had clubbed him, not knowing that Theresa lay awake by his side for a long time—staring with hatred into the darkness, savoring again the taste of her hand against his shrinking face, the crunching, bloody impact of the blow she had struck at all the men, the sly, beastly, snorting, sniveling, corrupt and corrupting men to whom she had had to give her body during and since the occupation.

Later, when Theresa fell asleep, Mueller began to toss. He dreamed that he went to Loringhoven's room at the Astoria and demanded his money and Loringhoven tried to throw him out. They fought, he subdued Loringhoven as easily as Theresa had subdued him, and he took the money. Not the money Loringhoven had promised him, but a whole suitcase of crisp new hundred-schilling notes.

Mueller awoke just before dawn. Theresa lay curled in a huge fetal ball, moaning.

He knew that he would have to go to Dieter Loringhoven after breakfast.

When the intermission lights went up in the Kursaal in Lucerne, Heinz Kemka noticed the Americans. One of them was a woman, a little on the attractive side.

The same afternoon, in Zum Wilden Mann, over a steaming crock of fondue, he had overheard them talking to Trudy.

He hadn't heard much, but Milo Hacha's name had been mentioned, and the name Longacre, Trudy's fly-by-night American lover. Although Trudy had since made overtures toward a reconciliation, Kemka was still smarting with jealousy. It would take her a long time to get back into his good graces. Besides, if these new Americans wished to find Longacre, and if Trudy did not want them to, and if in the same breath Milo Hacha's name had been mentioned . . .

Hadn't Trudy told him quite a lot about Milo Hacha?

Heinz Kemka smiled and sat down at the Americans' table.

"You liked the concert?"

"I loved it, Herr—?" the woman said.

"Kemka," Kemka said.

"Of course. How stupid of me. My name is Estelle Street and this is Mr. Goody."

"Hi-ya," Mr. Goody said in a bored voice.

"I hope you won't think this presumptuous of me, Madame—"

"Not at all. We're delighted to have you at our table."

"You see, I was lunching at Zum Wilden Mann this afternoon."

"A really splendid restaurant. You Swiss certainly do things with food."

". . . . And I couldn't help overhearing your conversation with Fräulein Ohlendorf."

The woman named Estelle Street suddenly seemed interested. "Yes, Herr Kemka?"

"Like Milo Hacha, I am a Czech. I believe I know where you can find him."

"Did you know Herr Hacha?"

"Let us say I know of him. Are you interested?"

"Yes. Of course we are. You see—" Estelle Street licked her lips and Kemka knew she was going to lie.

"Please. Don't trouble yourself telling me why."

"Well, that's fair enough," Estelle Street said.

"Good. Milo Hacha is employed by Cosmic Tours in Austria. Their main office, I believe, is in Vienna."

Estelle Street smiled. Even Mr. Goody looked almost happy. "Let me buy you a drink," the woman said.

"You are most kind, Madame."

Somehow that helped clean the slate. Already he felt much

better. In a day or two he might even condescend to take Trudy back.

"Man, I could really go for a shore dinner," Mr. Goody said. Heinz Kemka wondered what a shore dinner was. But he smiled just the same.

———————◆———————

14

How? How could it have gone wrong?

At least, Loringhoven told himself, Mueller had called from the lobby; that was something. It gave him a few moments to compose himself.

What if Mueller had barged right in? Mueller, who was supposed to be dead? He was not so foolish that he wouldn't have read the truth in the surprised look on Dieter Loringhoven's face, and then what?

Not that it had all gone wrong. The important thing was Hacha, and in that Dieter Loringhoven had not failed. Hacha was in Czechoslovakia, a lamb with dreams of glory. That was the important thing.

But Loringhoven's instructions had also called for the death of Hacha's guide. And the guide, very much alive, was now coming to claim his fee.

Dieter Loringhoven frowned. He was a small, slender man, and at first glance one would think the Slavic blood of eastern Austria had mixed with the German blood in his veins. But there was something Prussian about his appearance.

He carried himself very straight and despite his slenderness had a thick neck that bulged over his collar, supporting a round, almost shorn head.

His father, a Prussian from Brandenburg, had been killed in the Berlin riots of the twenties, when Brown Shirts and Communists terrorized all the cities of the Weimar Republic. His Viennese mother had survived until a smaller riot had claimed her life in Vienna on the eve of the *Anschluss*.

During the war, Dieter Loringhoven had been conscripted

from Brandenberg. The Nazis had used him as an *agent provocateur*, first in Austria, later in Hungary and Rumania. He saw no combat.

After the war he had gone back to Brandenburg, where he joined the Communist Party in 1948.

He did not believe in Communism as Communism; he was an opportunist who wanted to be carried along on what he considered to be the wave of the future.

The Communists, knowing his background and linguistic abilities, assigned him to the same sort of work the Nazis had taught him so well. Loringhoven had snooped for the Reds in Czechoslovakia and East Germany and he had uncovered and passed along the names of the leading organizers of the Poznan riot in Poland.

In some ways, the Hacha affair had been the most difficult of his career. True, the element of danger was lacking; he had only to convince Milo Hacha to return to Czechoslovakia. But it had taken him four whole months to do so.

Crafty and cynical himself, Hacha suspected everyone as as matter of course. Loringhoven had had to extend his acting talents to their outermost limits, displaying enthusiasm, respect, diffidence and even anger at psychological moments. And his own mounting curiosity had hampered his efforts.

The more he worked on Milo Hacha the harder he tried to learn why the Czechs wanted him—and why, wanting him, they didn't simply kidnap him and have done with it. Only two items in Hacha's past were suspect. His father had been a leader of the Czechoslovak Social Democrats, a hero, almost a martyr. And Hacha had been attached to the Gestapo on the Western Front during the war.

All this left Loringhoven confused and with no satisfying answers. But now, knocking at Loringhoven's door in the Hotel Astoria, presenting an immediate problem, was the guide who was supposed to be dead.

Loringhoven opened the door flashing his charming smile. "Come in, Mueller," he said. "Come in, come in."

He limped after Mueller into the living room. Mueller turned to face him. He was crumpling his hat and trying to control the quivering muscles around his mouth.

"Well, tell me all about it," Dieter Loringhoven said, as if he did not already know that Hacha had successfully crossed the border. "Has the new Assistant Minister of the Interior been sped on his way to Prague?"

Mueller mumbled an affirmative answer.

"Good," snapped Loringhoven. "The first the Czechs will know of it is when the next Five-Year Plan is announced from Prague by the new Assistant Minister, the son of a hero of the people—but, of course, this doesn't interest you. You came, naturally, for the money. But tell me at least what happened at the border. You were delayed? I expected you sooner."

"Siroky was gone," Mueller panted, as if he had run all the way upstairs. "I had to hide out—"

"Sit down," Loringhoven said compassionately. "Sit down, Mueller. You're shaking all over. Here's some brandy."

Mueller spilled half of it raising the glass to his lips. His fat face was chalky. "They shot at me," he stammered. "They tried to kill me, Herr Loringhoven. Even in the black-market days—may I have one more?" Loringhoven refilled the glass.

"Never again," Mueller said, "never again!" He drained the glass, and some color came into his cheeks.

"Well, it is over." Dieter Loringhoven bestowed another smile on him. "You have earned a bonus, you know."

The smile was contagious. Mueller began to smile, too. Soon his jowls were shaking, not with fear but with laughter.

Producing his billfold, Loringhoven took out a wad of hundred-schilling notes. "Fifteen hundred schillings," he said, counting them out on Mueller's lap. "You have earned it. A thousand schillings and a five-hundred schilling bonus. Well done!"

Mueller seemed astounded. He stuffed the money into his pocket and jumped out of the chair.

"Danke, Herr Loringhoven. *Danke schon!"*

"We must have a drink some time together when next I am in Vienna."

"You are leaving, Herr Loringhoven?"

"But of course. My business here is finished." He ushered Mueller to the door. "I wish to thank you for a splendid achievement."

A grin bisected Mueller's face, making it look fatter. He punched Loringhoven's shoulder with his pudgy left fist. Loringhoven winced. He detested physical contact.

"Yes, yes, yes," Mueller babbled, pumping Loringhoven's hand up and down. "Yes, yes—"

He patted the pocket in which the money was stuffed, then staggered out into the hall.

Dieter Loringhoven shut the door and looked at the hand that Mueller had pumped. He went into the bathroom and washed his hands thoroughly with soap and hot water. When he had dried them, he flung the contaminated towel on the floor.

Then he lit a cigarette, picked up the telephone and gave the operator a number.

"Ja, bitte?" a voice answered.

"This is Pilsen Brandenburg."

"Ja, Herr Brandenburg?"

"Gerhard Mueller. He is a bus driver for Cosmic Tours. Their office is on The Graben. When in Vienna Mueller lives at Praterstrasse 178."

"Ja, Herr Brandenburg?"

"Liquidate him," Dieter Loringhoven said.

The impersonal voice said, *"Jawohl."*

———◆———

15

"But I can tell you this," Theresa said in her surprisingly good English. "Maybe he'll lead you to the border. Maybe he'll tell you where Milo Hacha went. But he'll never take you across. You couldn't get him to take you across now for a million schillings."

"I don't know this schilling business," Steve Longacre said. "There's five hundred bucks in it for him. You know, dollars."

"It's not enough," Gerhard Mueller's mistress said. "No amount would be enough. But perhaps, Mr. Longacre, he would lead you *to* the border and tell you how to get across by yourself."

"That's no good, Fräulein," Steve said.

Theresa shrugged. "Then perhaps Gerhard could arrange to have you taken across the border by someone else. He has connections. But it would cost you more money."

"How much more?"

"That you would have to arrange with Gerhard. Cigarette?"

Steve nodded, frowning. Just then the door crashed open and Gerhard Mueller rushed into the room. "I got the money, *liebchen*," he cried in German. "You see, I got it. Not one thousand, but fifteen hundred—ah, Herr Longacre!"

Theresa took the money and counted it. "Herr Longacre still wants to go after the Czech," she said in German. "Can you arrange it? I think that he will pay."

"I'm not going back there," Gerhard Mueller whined.

"Who said anything about going back, stupid? I said, can you arrange it?"

"*Ja, ja*, it is possible. I know a trucker—"

"Don't sound so eager, you fool. You must act doubtful. He will pay more."

But Mueller's thoughts were elsewhere. "Loringhoven was friendly," he said. "He was actually grateful! What a fool I was."

Theresa glared at him and turned to Steve. "Gerhard thinks there is a possibility it can be arranged," she said in English. "But as you Americans say, there will be many palms to be greased."

"You talk my lingo pretty good," Steve growled.

"The war taught us many things, Mr. Longacre," Theresa said, shrugging. She had lived with an American sergeant for two years in the American zone. When the sergeant shipped out, she had moved over to Praterstrasse with a Russian captain. She knew the colloquial expression for bribery in Russian, too.

"Can you afford five thousand schillings? It may cost you even more."

Steve rose. "Let's stop playing hi'-go-seek, Fräulein. You find out if he can do it and what it'll cost, then let me know. But it's got to be soon. Kapeesh?"

"What does he say?" Mueller asked in German.

"He is in a hurry, Gerhard. He is going to pay. Almost anything we want to ask!"

There was a rap on the door.

Steve looked at the big blonde suspiciously. "Expecting somebody?"

"Not I—"

"Do not answer," Mueller whispered. He was chalk-faced again. "Theresa, no!"

But she was striding over to the door. *"Feigling,"* she said contemptuously. "The so-called men I pick!"

She opened the door. A man and a woman stood there.

"Ja?" Theresa said blankly.

But both visitors were looking past Theresa to Steve Longacre.

"Hi-ya, Stevie boy," the man said.

It was Lou Goody, who had driven the getaway car the night they killed Joey Imparato.

The woman was Estelle Street.

When Theresa drove Gerhard Mueller in her battered Citroën from the Praterstrasse to the Wagramer Bridge across the Danube, Mueller crept out of the car and scurried for the nearest shadow. He watched her drive off with longing and hatred. Why did he let her dominate him so? The fifteen hundred hadn't been enough for her. No, she had to have more . . . always more. . . .

Mueller used his sleeve to wipe his face. It came away soaked.

He scampered down the cobblestone ramp, glancing frequently over his shoulder. Everything was quiet, so very quiet, tonight. He found himself trying to hurry on tiptoe. It was impossible; he had weak ankles and flat feet. An elephant lumbering through the jungle could not be noisier, he thought in agony. Suddenly a monstrous roar overwhelmed him; he stopped, transfixed, expecting to die. But it was only a late suburban train going by, with blobs of faces in the yellow windows. If only he were on it!

Mueller wiped his face again and hurried on.

When he saw the truck parked in the shadow of the deserted market under the bridge he almost sobbed with relief. It was the right one, no doubt about that, a big Diesel-driven cab with two trailer vans. Or was it? He stole closer, straining his eyes. Yes! There were the words BUD-WEISER PILSEN on the sides of both vans.

Mueller sneaked up to the cab. "Helmut?" he called softly. If it was not Helmut he would run . . . run. . . .

But it was Helmut; the tall man with the bald spot and thin, dark face swinging down to the curb was unmistakable.

"Gerhard!" he said warmly, seizing Mueller's hand. "I still

can't believe it. I thought you'd given up the black-market business. There's no profit in it now."

"For God's sake, lower your voice, Helmut!"

"We're safe enough," the truck driver said. "Ah, those good old black-market days. The money we made, hey, Gerhard?"

"And the money we spent," Mueller muttered, wiping his face again. "I don't remember when I've suffered from the heat so much. . . . Anyway, I'm through with the black market. Why the devil don't they come?" He kept searching the dark street. "Helmut, you're sure—?"

"Relax," Helmut said comfortably. "There's nothing illegal about driving a truck of Budweiser. I believe, Gerhard, you mentioned something about two thousand schillings . . . ?"

Mueller handed him an envelope containing twenty hundred-schilling notes, still looking around nervously. The truck driver opened the envelope and counted the bills with concentration and growing satisfaction. Mueller wondered what his friend would say if he knew that Herr Longacre had slipped him three thousand schillings and the other two Americans—the man and the woman whose names he never did learn—had given him three thousand schillings, also. Two from six left four, four thousand schillings clear profit . . . which Theresa, of course, had promptly taken charge of. . . . Where, where were the Americans?

"I take your three clients as far as Ceske Budejovice," Helmut said, stowing the money away. "That is correct?"

"Only two of them," Mueller mumbled. "Helmut, you have the motorcycle?"

"In the second van, Gerhard. With a sidecar, as you said."

"Good. The third American, a woman, goes only as far as the border. I'll take her back."

"A woman?" Helmut said. He seemed unpleasantly surprised. He gave Mueller a cigarette and lit one for himself. "I'm not sure I like that."

"What difference does it make? You drop us off this side of the border. Where *are* they!"

"And the two men?"

"When they're ready to come back, they'll make contact with you in Pilsen."

"And if I don't happen to be in Pilsen—?"

"They'll wait until you are. That's not your problem."

"And it's understood they're to pay me two thousand more when I sneak them back into Austria?"

"Yes."

Helmut said suddenly, "Someone is coming."

Mueller's heart jumped. He dropped his unsmoked cigarette and peered. Then he let out his breath with relief. The two figures emerging from the darkness were the American couple whose names he did not know.

The man had a Luger in his hand. "Mueller?"

"*Ja, ja.*"

"Very fine," Helmut said, "Oh, very fine! I'm to take an armed man across. You didn't tell me that, Gerhard. For God's sake, tell him to hide that thing."

"I don't speak English," Mueller said fretfully, still searching the shadows, "and he doesn't speak German."

Helmut swore. But the woman said something to the man, and the weapon disappeared.

So she understood German, Mueller thought. She had not indicated that at their meeting. For some reason the fact increased his nervousness. "What did you say, Helmut?"

"I said, do they have papers?" Helmut said sullenly.

"I got two sets from Fritz Severing."

"Severing? Are you out of your—?"

"Wait, Helmut, come over here," Mueller whispered hastily, glancing at the Americans. They were a few yards off, hugging the first van, looking up the street. "The woman apparently knows German. Keep your voice down."

"Severing's forged papers are no good. They wouldn't fool a cockeyed Czech guard with a liter of vodka under his belt on Red Army Day!"

"It was the best I could do."

"And if they're caught?"

"Then you won't have to take them back."

"And I'll lose that extra two thousand!"

Gerhard Mueller began to feel irritated. "So you'll lose it. Look, Helmut, you know the risks in this sort of affair—"

"Sure. And they could implicate me, too!"

Mueller controlled himself. If Helmut lost his nerve. . . . He managed to say, good-humoredly, "Who's acting like an old woman now? It's all right, Helmut. Nothing's going to go wrong."

"You should have told me, that's all," the truck driver

grumbled. "Why do they want to go to Czechoslovakia, anyway?"

"I don't know," Mueller said carelessly. "They're looking for someone. Something like that."

"Who?"

"What difference does it make?"

"Who's that?"

Both men stiffened, listening intently.

"It must be Herr Longacre," Mueller muttered. "Yes!"

Steve, wearing soiled corduroy trousers and a cheap wool workman's shirt like the other male American, came into view. He said something curtly to the man and the woman and strode over to the two Austrians. "This the driver, Mueller? Oh, you don't savvy English, do you? All right, let's get rolling, quickly. What the hell is that word? *Schnell, schnell."*

The woman said in halting German, "Tell us what to do, please."

"You will hide in here," Helmut said. He began to open the sliding door in the side of the first van behind the cab. Over his shoulder he said to Mueller, "I haven't been paid for the motorcycle."

"You'll get it back, Helmut. And don't forget. I get off with the woman at Gmünd. No nearer the border than Gmünd."

"You take a lot of chances, don't you?" the driver said sourly. He pointed into the van with urgency.

Gerhard Mueller could hear the Danube lapping against its banks and a tram rumbling by overhead on the Wagramer Bridge, as the three Americans climbed in. He was about to climb in after them when a man's voice came out of the cobbled darkness.

"Wait! Steve! Steve?"

The man was running. He will be heard in Prague, Mueller thought despairingly.

Helmut cursed. "Now what?"

"It's all right. I think it is Herr Longacre's young brother—"

"Nothing was said about another one!"

"I know. It's some misunderstanding. . . ."

The two Americans already in the van stuck their heads out. The armed one had his Luger showing again. He said something in an angry voice to Herr Longacre. Herr Longacre seemed apologetic and unhappy.

The young man who came running up, puffing, was indeed Herr Longacre's brother. If only I could understand their *verdammlich* tongue! Mueller thought.

The brothers were shouting at each other. Helmut seemed ready to bolt. The woman appeared. She spoke to the man with the Luger. The man with the Luger spoke sharply to Herr Longacre. Herr Longacre shook his head. The young man now stopped shouting at Herr Longacre and was speaking to the woman. She listened, considered, nodded. Immediately the three already in the van retreated into the black interior.

So the woman is running things, Mueller thought. That was an unpleasant development of an already unpleasant night. He wiped his face for the third time.

"Listen," the younger Longacre said to Mueller in German. "She wants me to go along. She says it's all right."

"You have papers?" Mueller said.

"I have an American passport."

"But no Czech visa."

"I can speak German. I'll do them more good than harm."

"Can you speak the Czech language?"

"No. But there are plenty of Sudeten Czechs who can't either."

"Let him come, let him come," Helmut groaned. "How long are we going to stand here? But this will cost them an extra thousand on the return trip!"

The Diesel engine roared. The truck drove up the ramp and turned right, across the Wagramer Bridge.

Ten minutes later they recrossed the Danube on the Jagerstrasse Bridge, and five minutes after that they were rumbling north through the quiet suburbs toward the Czech frontier.

———◆———

16

At first there was little talking in the van.

Every few minutes Estelle Street would ask anxiously, "What time is it, Lou?" A match would be struck and in its puff of light Andy could see Steve's face dimly and Lou Goody's face clearly.

Goody looked worried. In the stifling heat of the van's interior, his face glistened with sweat. As far as Andy could tell, Steve looked more angry than concerned.

Then suddenly Estelle Street said, "What are you so nervous about, Lou?"

"Who wouldn't be nervous?" Goody said. "You realize where we're headed for, Mrs. Street? That's one bunch of tough babies over there."

"You picked a fine time to think of that," she snapped. "And here I was under the impression that you're the tough baby." Her voice sweetened. "It's just another job, Lou. The kind of job you've done—how many times is it? Relax."

"Yeah," Goody muttered. "Relax."

Andy wondered what the expression on Steve's face was now. Steve was being awfully quiet.

They all sat in silence for awhile.

Then Goody said, "I sure as hell wish Bigger was here."

"I'm beginning to wish the same thing," Estelle said sarcastically.

"Making himself scarce all of a sudden," Goody complained. "I should be so smart. He's prob'ly down in Miami or some place having himself a ball. Damn it, I wish we'd located him!"

"Oh, shut up," she said. "The ten grand you're going to get ought to stiffen your backbone long enough to pull a trigger."

So there it is, Andy thought. That's what Steve had been keeping from him, why they had come to Europe in the first place. They were there to find Milo Hacha, all right— to find him and kill him. Andy wondered why he felt so little sense of shock. But then he realized that, buried far down somewhere, he had known it all along.

No wonder Steve was being so quiet.

All at once it came back to Andy—who Lou Goody was. He had seen his picture in the papers once, along with the picture of a much bigger man. The big man's name was Biggert, but they called him Bigger.

He was a hood, and so was Lou Goody, hangers-on from the old strong-arm days in Long Island County. Barney Street's goons.

Andy's muscles felt stiff and cramped. When the truck

had started he had crouched down against the tail gate of the van and hadn't moved since. Now he got up and almost fell as the van rolled over some hole in the road.

"What's the matter, kid?" Steve said. If the question was innocuous, the voice that asked it told a long story.

"Nothing," Andy said.

Milo Hacha, he thought. I don't even know what you look like. But here are two pretty good boys, proficient at their trade, come four thousand miles to bump you off. One of them is my brother. And they're not going to leave Czechoslovakia till you're dead.

Andy's thoughts continued to drift in the sweltering darkness. What would Trudy have done if she had known that this was why they were looking for Milo Hacha? And then there was Milo Hacha's daughter in Holland, and the dead old man who had convinced himself that the girl was his granddaughter. The heat and the strong smell of beer in the van made him thirsty. Or was his mouth dry because he was afraid?

The truck suddenly ground to a stop. They waited in silence. Mueller went cautiously to the door of the van. Finally, it slid open. "Gmünd," Helmut's voice said. It cracked with urgency.

Mueller launched himself out of the van's darkness into the darkness of the road. He had not uttered a sound during the trip.

But now he thrust his head into the van and shrilled, "Herr Longacre, the woman. Tell her she must get out at once!"

"This is where you get off, Mrs. Street," Andy said. "He says to hurry."

"Ten thousand dollars," Estelle Street's voice said. "Remember, Lou."

"Okay, okay."

"I'm depending on you, too, Steve. I don't have to remind you what it means to—well, let's say to both of us."

Steve sounded as if he were strangling. "Will you get the hell out of here?"

Estelle jumped out of the van like a gazelle. Lou Goody lit another cigarette. In the flare of the match Andy saw Steve glaring at him in a sort of agony. Then the match went out.

It wouldn't be money in Steve's case, Andy thought.

Steve didn't need money. It sounded like something else. Something nasty. She had a hold on Steve. A death grip.

The tail gate of the rear van came clanking down. A few moments later an engine exploded into life. Andy poked his head out. The moon had risen, or come out from behind a cloud; in its soft light he saw a motorcycle with a side-car speeding up the road in the direction from which they had come. The tail gate clanked back.

Then Helmut's big hand was grasping the edge of the door. Andy pulled his head in.

Seconds later, they were once more under way.

The woman was a type, Gerhard Mueller decided.

Another woman would have scrunched down in the side-car behind the windshield. This one sat calm and straight, letting the wind tumble her hair about. She was attractive but hard-looking, and in the moonlight he could see that her lips were parted in a smile of sheer sensuality.

Well, so she was a strange one. What was it to him? Mueller was feeling good. Good indeed. His work was over. He had done his part, to the letter, and Dieter Loring-hoven's fifteen hundred schillings had multiplied astoundingly.

True, Theresa was holding the money. But he had earned it and they would spend it together. There was that about Theresa. Money for her, as for him, was to be spent. Not like his wife who, a lower-class *Hausfrau*, a peasant really, begrudged every groschen.

Headlights blinded him suddenly. The American woman shouted. Mueller barely heard her over the roar of the motorcycle's engine.

What was the damn fool trying to do, run them down?

Mueller wrenched the handle bars and the motorcycle swerved with its sidecar toward the soft shoulder of the road. He fought frantically to control the vehicle, vaguely aware that the car responsible for their plight had jammed to a stop a few yards away.

The motorcycle hurtled over on its side. The American woman was flung out. She landed heavily on Mueller. "You God damn clumsy *oaf!*"

Mueller disentangled himself slowly. By a miracle he was unhurt. He helped the cursing woman to her feet. She cried out, and he saw that she was standing with one foot off the ground, like an injured dog.

Mueller fumed. This would have to happen just as everything was working like a charm! He briefly considered thrashing the driver of the car. But the man climbing out of it looked rather large. Anyway, Mueller told himself, he would need the idiot's help. Perhaps the motorcycle was wrecked. In that case . . .

Mueller peered. He could not make out the man well. The rascal was standing in the shadow of the dark sedan. He seemed very large indeed. Mueller decided to be generous.

"These things happen, *mein Herr,*" he called in a man-to-man voice. "If you'll be kind enough to help me with my motorcycle. . . . ?"

The woman was clinging to him, moaning. Mueller took a step toward the car, assisting her. The man had not moved.

"Mein Herr?" Mueller said again.

The man spoke. "Gerhard Mueller?"

Mueller's heart leaped like a fish. The man knew his name. How could that be?

Bewildered, Gerhard Mueller watched the man's arms appear from the shadow. They seemed to be holding something.

"I am Gerhard Mueller. But how—?"

Then he saw what it was.

Mueller felt the surge of a great desire to run, to run. But something seemed to have happened to his legs. And there was the woman clinging to him, oblivious to everything but her pain. I will scream, Mueller thought. But his throat was paralyzed, too.

I will call out to Theresa, waiting for me in the apartment on the Praterstrasse. I will say, see, I did it, I did it, I did it for us, *liebchen,* I earned all that money for us. . . .

Very vividly Mueller saw the apartment, the dear apartment, the beautiful old sofa with its frilly antimacassars, the stylish Hungarian lamp with its lovely orange globe, Theresa, the beloved, wearing the new leather coat he had decided they were going to buy for her. . . .

It was a machine pistol.

That was when Gerhard Mueller's throat came unstuck and he uttered a great scream and he felt the muscles of his legs come to life, but fire was coming out of the machine pistol and immeasurable agony sprayed across his well-filled stomach to the accompaniment of a loud chatter, as of a thousand typewriters, and then Mueller felt and heard nothing more. . . .

For a moment the man looked down at the quiet bodies of Gerhard Mueller and Estelle Street, tumbled together in the intimate integration of death, then he climbed into his car and drove a little way down the road to swing out and back and out again, past the two bodies once more as he settled contentedly down to the long drive back to Vienna and the successful report he must make to Herr Pilsen Brandenburg.

Part FIVE

FIVE

Milo Hacha

———•———

17

From Andy Longacre's diary:

. . . funny thing about it was that for a time I assumed Milo Hacha was as good as dead, simply because Steve and Lou Goody were gunning for him.

Actually, it's hard to pinpoint when the change in my thinking occurred. When it did, I went too far in the other direction.

But first things first. When I thought it through, I realized that the sending of Steve and Lou Goody to Czechoslovakia to murder Milo Hacha wasn't too far from the classical *modus operandi* of gangland slayings. In a gangland slaying, the local talent is rarely used. The reason's obvious: if out-of-town killers are brought in, they stand less chance of being identified.

Ideally, the out-of-towner meets the finger man, who identifies the victim for him, does the job as soon as possible and blows right out again.

The one thing missing in our setup was a finger man. Since none of us knew what Milo Hacha looked like or where we could find him, the lack of a finger man could be serious.

Beside this, we had to cross an international border twice without being seen. And it looked like the kind of mob-type hit Lou Goody and Steve could handle.

Then I got to thinking. Steve and Lou Goody couldn't speak a word of anything but English and I couldn't touch Czechoslovak although I spoke German and Russian well enough. The trucker, who turned out to be a big hunk of chicken, would only take us as far as a town called Ceske Budejovice, less than a quarter of the way from the border to Prague. Prague was a city of a million people. Assuming we ever got that far, we'd have to find Hacha somehow without arousing suspicion, do our job and get out before they started looking for us. Also, Steve gave us the low-down in the truck as he'd gotten it from Mueller.

Milo Hacha had been invited back to Czechoslovakia to assume the post of Assistant Minister of the Interior. In other words, a front man. This was to be a surprise and a delight for the burghers of Prague, who still revered Milo's old man, Rudolf, one of their former Social Democrat leaders in the pre-Communist days. That being the case, Hacha would probably be kept under wraps until the Reds decided it was time to spring their surprise. Then how could we hope to find him?

Steve and Lou Goody were huddled together, talking a mile a minute. I didn't pay much attention to them. Goody was a semi-stupid thug dreaming of ten thousand American bucks and Steve was scared. That left me to do the straight thinking, if any was to be done. The way I saw it, we stood our best chance of returning to Austria in an upright position if we didn't go anywhere near Milo Hacha. I came to that conclusion just before we reached the border. So I decided to get us caught without entrance visas before we even set foot on Czech soil.

It seemed a shame. I did want to meet Milo Hacha face to face. I really did. Henry M. Stanley seeking Dr. Living-stone all over central Africa couldn't have felt worse about it than I did. Hacha had become the pivot around which my life swung. I can't say why.

Anyway, I was going to blow the whole thing on the border, and the hell with Estelle Street.

"Hey, we're slowing down," Lou Goody said.

The big trailer truck rolled to a stop, its brakes squeaking. For a while nothing happened, then Andy heard boots thudding on concrete. He was tense and ready; he had made up his mind. If he was going to do anything to keep them out of Czechoslovakia, he had to do it now.

Andy got to his feet and walked over to the side door of the van. He could hear voices faintly, Helmut saying something and one of the guards answering. Then the truck driver laughed and the guard laughed.

"Keep still, kid," Steve's voice said in his ear. Andy hadn't heard Steve approach at all. He felt his brother's hand on his arm. Andy drew back his foot.

That was when Lou Goody grabbed him from behind. It had to be Goody, because Steve was still breathing in his ear. Goody's arm whipped around Andy's neck, crooked and pulled back hard. Andy's brain said, yell! and he yelled like mad; only nothing came out. Also, nothing was going in. A fire started in his lungs and the van began to spin, slowly at first, then faster and faster.

"All right, Lou, all right, Lou," Steve's voice was saying from far away. "He's out on his feet. Let go. . . ."

Goody let go. Andy opened his mouth like an autointoxicated fish, half-turning in a stagger. That was when the edge of Goody's hand hit him in the Adam's apple, a sharp, precise chop. Darkness fell, a darker darkness.

He opened his eyes to find himself lying on the floor of the van. His neck, throat . . .

Goody's voice was saying in a whisper, "Look, Steve, brother or no brother, the son of a bitch was trying to get us caught. What was I supposed to do, kiss him?"

Steve's voice was not there. But Steve's hands were. One was over Andy's mouth. The other was gently massaging Andy's neck.

The truck began to roll.

Into Czechoslovakia.

Andy was sitting propped up against the side wall of the van feeling all sorts of miseries. The sizzling roar of the trailer truck, the stifling heat inside the van, made the moment a timeless nightmare.

A new sound obtruded. Like a punching bag in action. Andy opened his eyes, narrowed them in the murk. Lou Goody was tattooing the front wall of the van with both fists.

"What do you think you're doing?" Andy heard Steve ask.

"You just keep watching that wise-guy brother of yours," Lou shouted back. He kept pounding away.

The truck began to slow down. Finally, it stopped.

"What's the idea?" Steve demanded.

"That's just what, Steve. An idea." Goody went to the side

door. It slid open a foot or two. Helmut's face appeared in the moonlight, alarmed.

"What is it? What's wrong?" Helmut asked in German.

"You—Andy," Goody said. "Tell him I want to ride up front with him."

Andy glanced at Steve. Steve said nothing. Andy said to Helmut in German, "This man wishes to get into the cab with you."

The driver shook his head violently, began to slide the door shut. Lou Goody's foot stopped it.

"Tell the slug there ain't gonna be no arguments." The Luger was suddenly pointing at Helmut's head.

"I think," Andy said, in English, "Helmut has seen the eternal truth of your position. Translation unnecessary."

Helmut disappeared. Goody jumped into the road. He shut the door. A few seconds later the truck resumed its journey.

The brothers rode along in silence for a long time.

Suddenly Andy said, "Is Goody the boss or are you?"

"It's not a question of boss," Steve said.

"Then why did you let him go up front? That's pretty stupid, Steve. We're deep in Czechoslovakia. Suppose Helmut is stopped?"

"Look who's talking," Steve said. "Andy. What were you trying to pull?"

"It's a long and very complicated story, Steve," Andy said wearily. "The story of a thought process. Forget it."

"Oh, yeah? My own brother? Look, kid." Steve moved over and squatted beside Andy. "It's probably my fault. I should have leveled with you. Only, well, I sort of didn't want you to know what kind of a horse's patoot you had for a brother."

"I know, Steve," Andy said.

"You know from nothing!" Steve said in a choked voice. "You think I'm doing all this for dough? Estelle Street's dough?"

"No. I know you don't need her blood-money."

"Barney Street left all his dough to this Hacha. Estelle wants it. To get it, she has to have Hacha dead."

"That much I figured out for myself."

"Okay, you're a brain. Here's the part you couldn't figure." Steve paused. Then he said, very fast, "Once, kid, I killed a man. At least I was there with the man who did, which legally boils down to the same thing. Estelle found out. She can strap me in the chair and pull the switch on me any time she chooses. That's why I'm on this junket. I tried to keep you out of it. I'll never forgive myself for letting you con me into taking you along. My only excuse is I kept telling myself Hacha must be dead already. . . . That stunt of yours, trying to get us stopped at the border, it might have meant curtains for me. From here on in I got to leave it up to you."

Andy felt a spreading weariness. For no reason at all he could suddenly think only of that night when he had gotten drunk for the first time in his life and Steve had beaten him up like a maniac, a maniac with tears streaming down his cheeks.

He felt a little like crying now himself.

Andy became dimly aware that the truck was slowing to a stop.

"Listen, kid," Steve was saying eagerly. "We'll go away somewhere afterward. Start over. Some place like Brazil, say. A guy who doesn't mind a little hard work can live like a king down there. What do you say, kid? Is it a deal? . . . Andy?"

After a while Steve put his head between his hands.

It was then that Andy heard the shot.

They both jumped like one man to the side door. Steve wrestled with it, cursing. Then the door slid back and Andy saw Lou Goody's face in the moonlight. It was afraid and defiant at the same time.

"Lou," Steve said sharply. "What happened?" He stuck his head out and looked up and down the road. Andy looked, too. Nothing. "I said what happened, Lou!"

Lou licked his lips. Steve jumped down, shook Goody roughly. The night was dry and hot. A slight wind stirred Andy's hair. Crickets were chirping in a field across the way, a field full of twisted, skinny poles. A hops field, Andy thought. He got stiffly down in the road.

"I had me this brainstorm," Lou Goody mumbled. "Why should we get off at this Chesky-whatever-the-hell-it-is? I got it across to this slob of a driver, in sign lingo mostly. And I keep on saying, 'Prague, Prague.' He starts in jabbering away a mile a minute, sore as hell. All right, so maybe it was a lousy idea, Steve. But he's got no business grabbing a tire iron and making like he's gonna swing on me."

"You shot him," Steve said in an unbelieving voice.

"I didn't mean to, Steve," Goody whined. "I just thought I'd scare him into behaving himself. Instead, he tries to muscle the gun away from me and it goes off."

"How bad is he?" Steve barked.

Lou Goody made a slight backward movement, uneasily. "He's dead."

Steve stared at him. Then, without a word, he went over to the cab of the truck and looked in. Andy followed.

Helmut lay over the wheel. His open eyes were looking right at Andy.

Andy found himself crouching against the side of the cab, retching.

Lou Goody and Steve had already pulled the body out and over to the other side of the road and were going through the clothing, removing papers and identifying marks and his wallet. Then Goody fished some cotton waste from under the front seat and cleaned up the cab. He went back to the other side of the road and helped Steve lug the dead man into the hops field. They were gone about five minutes. Steve boosted Andy into the cab and climbed in after him.

Goody was already behind the wheel.

"Nothing to it, Steve," he said soothingly, looking over the dashboard. "You know there ain't nothing on wheels I can't drive."

"Get rolling," Steve said.

"Come on, Steve," Goody said. "You think I wanted to kill the slob?"

"Shut up!"

"Steve—"

"Drive."

Outside Ceske Bodejovice the truck's headlights picked up the first highway marker to Prague.

18

Professor Vaclav Mydlár, Minister of the Interior of the People's Democratic Republic of Czechoslovakia, smiled. He was a squirrelly little man with bushy white hair, bright eyes and fat cheeks. "Out of the woodwork of Prague," he said, "will come all the old Social Democrats. I'll admit it, at first I thought the government had summoned you as an *agent provocateur*. But now—" Another smile. "You must forgive me for running on like this, Milo."

"It's quite all right," Milo Hacha said. "I'm interested in everything you can tell me. I need to learn. I want to learn."

"Well, I will tell you," Professor Mydlár said. "I managed to survive, as your revered father did not. Nominally, I am a Communist." He looked quizzical. "That was something Rudolf Hacha could never bring himself to become. But there are many of us old Social Democrats—Hodza, Nosek, Bormann. I could compile quite a list, my boy. In the woodwork now, but ready to come out. Because you are here, Milo. Because the Party admitted, in bringing back a Hacha, that we were necessary."

Professor Mydlár scowled. "At first I thought, it's a trick. Provocation, the usual thing. But they haven't boarded you up in an obscure ministry somewhere, out of things. They need us, don't you see, if they are to maintain power. That's why they let you come here to live, a free man, in my house. My boy, given time, it will be a revolution!"

"I'd rather you didn't talk like that, Professor," Milo Hacha said. "I'm not the least interested in starting a revolution. The government offered me a post as your assistant. That's the only reason I came."

Professor Mydlár tried to hide his disappointment. There was so much that Hacha did not know, so much he did not seem to want to know.

Mydlár was an old man, almost seventy. The only alternative to weak parliamentary democracy was strong parliamentary democracy. Strong parliamentary democracy protected the state while leaving the individual intact. It had taken Vaclav Mydlár a lifetime of disillusionments to learn it.

Could he impart this great truth to a naïve Milo Hacha in a few evenings talk? No, it was better not to try.

The professor smiled. "Here in Prague we have a symbol, my boy."

"A symbol?" Milo Hacha seemed faintly wary.

"Yes, the Manes Café here in the Malá Strana. It was there that the old political idealists used to meet. It is there, if anywhere, that a new Czechoslovakia will be born. It is there, in the Manes Café, that you will meet the old friends of your father. It is arranged. Tomorrow night . . ."

The old man rambled on. He's hopelessly lost somewhere in a cuckoo land. Milo Hacha's thoughts drifted to Mydlár's Libusé. Named after the heroine of a patriotic bourgeois opera. Very romantic, Hacha thought. But that was her father's doing. The flesh-and-blood Libusé Mydlár, with her neglected raven's hair, her grimly pretty face that scorned make-up, was underfed, had a shapely and grimly efficient body. . . . Grim. Yes, grim was the word for her.

Libusé came in now, wearing a severe gray dress, to clear the dinner dishes while her father wandered comfortably through his dreamland. She won't look at me, Milo Hacha thought. Suddenly he thought, she hates me.

". . . Masaryk," the old man said.

Was it a test? Milo Hacha wondered. Had the Party sent him here to live with this old fool and his daughter as a test?

It was unexpected, this girl Libusé's hatred. Whatever else Hacha lacked, he knew it was not unattractiveness to women. He liked to think of himself as a Villon, a Casanova with principles—the hero, perhaps, of a rogue novel. Principles . . . He almost laughed aloud as old Mydlár prattled on.

He thought back to his time in the Netherlands, where circumstances had made him a hero. With the war almost over and the Nazis obviously beaten, he had helped some Allied flyers escape. Why? Who knew the reasons for such things? Perhaps he had dreamed of someday going to England. Or to America. Certainly it had not been a matter of principles.

They had woven a legend around him, untrue though flattering. He might have stayed on, but the woman, the mayor's wife, had become troublesome. So he had left the Netherlands. It was too bad about the child. Such a pretty little thing.

S---itzerland? Trudy, he thought. He remembered Trudy's body, her abandon, with regret. In Switzerland he had lived as a gentleman-gambler. The classic rogue. But Trudy had engulfed him in her astonishing passion. Drowning, he had had to move on.

And Austria? That was a comedown, indeed. Passenger representative for a bus line. Hardly more than a tourist guide! And the tourists themselves—how he had grown to hate them, with their gaucherie, their cameras, their inane questions!

His interlude in the wilderness. Waiting for what was to come.

And now? Back to Czechoslovakia and glory! If this doddering Professor Mydlár thought Milo Hacha was going to stick his neck out, get involved in intrigues and revolution . . .

Was it a test?

". . . an old man," Vaclav Mydlár said, smiling. "Forgive me, but I am going to bed. Why don't you children get acquainted?"

Children!

The Professor shook hands formally and left. Hacha was alone with Libusé. He wondered with amusement what her tack would be.

"Do you have a cigarette, Herr Hacha?" she asked abruptly. She spoke in German as though she refused to regard him except as a visiting alien.

He gave her a cigarette and lit it for her. "I wanted to talk to you," she said in her flat, mannish voice. Her gaunt face was expressionless. She stood very straight, like a soldier.

"Yes, of course." He spoke in Czech, holding a chair out for her.

She continued in German, quite as if he had not spoken at all.

"What I have to say, Herr Hacha, can be said standing up. It is this. My father is an old man. He has been hurt greatly in his life. He was forced to watch the Nazis torture my brother Woodrow to death."

Woodrow, Milo Hacha thought. The son named for the man who had made the Czechoslovakian state a reality, the daughter named for the national heroine. By such childishness they had tried to roll back the Communist tide!

"Your father was Father's best friend," Libusé went on.

"But he testified against your father at his trial because he believed it to be in the best interests of a strong and unified Czechoslovakia. For your father it did not matter. He was going to die in either case. The mistake—and it was a mistake—broke my father's spirit. Now he lives on one hope."

"Yes?" Milo Hacha asked politely.

"You. Don't disappoint him, Herr Hacha." She ground her cigarette out in a saucer. "If you do, I shall surely kill you."

She stalked from the room.

19

Dieter Loringhoven's telephone rang just after two in the morning.

"*Ja?*"

"Pilsen Brandenburg, *bitte*."

"This is he."

"The job is done, Herr Brandenburg."

"Splendid."

"But there are complications." First the assassin told Dieter Loringhoven about the woman with Mueller. Then about the Budweiser trailer truck that had been carrying Mueller's motorcycle.

"Where was this?" Loringhoven asked.

"Near Gmünd, on the road to the Czech border."

"Did they cross?"

"I don't know, Herr Brandenburg. I didn't follow them."

Dieter Loringhoven hung up and thought about it. Assuming the truck had crossed into Czechoslovakia, and it seemed likely, did that necessarily indicate a connection with the Hacha affair? It might.

Loringhoven dressed carefully. He drove to the Praterstrasse and rapped peremptorily on Theresa's door. She opened it, knuckling the sleep out of her puffed eyes. There was a transparent wrapper over her nightgown.

"You are the woman who lives with Gerhard Mueller?"

She was awake instantly. "What do you want?"

"I am from the police."

She stood aside, mouth open. Loringhoven went in.

"Wait," Theresa said. She ran into the other room. He waited patiently in the ugly bourgeois living room. She returned wearing a dress and carrying two cups of coffee. She offered him one of the cups, mutely. He ignored it.

"I must tell you," Loringhoven snapped, "that your man is in trouble."

She was watching him warily over the rim of her cup.

"Who accompanied Mueller to the border?"

"The border?" she said. "I know nothing of any border."

Loringhoven stared at her. Theresa's glance fell. "I really don't know what you're talking about, Sir," she said into her cup.

Loringhoven shrugged. "Very well," he said. He limped to the door.

"That's . . . all?"

"Hardly, Fräulein. We take long looks at persons who refuse to assist us. Good night!" He put his hand on the doorknob.

"Wait," she said. "Wait, please!"

Loringhoven turned around. "But if you don't know what I'm talking about, you can't help me."

"Where is Gerhard?"

"Detained."

"At the border?"

"What have you to tell me, Fräulein?" Loringhoven came back into the room and picked up the other coffee cup.

The silence lengthened. Dieter Loringhoven did nothing to disturb it. He looked at his wristwatch and then at the woman. He said nothing.

"Gerhard went with some Americans to the Czechoslovakian border."

Loringhoven finished his coffee. "So? Why?"

"I don't know," she mumbled.

He chuckled. "My dear Theresa, don't you think we know all about Milo Hacha? And that Mueller took Hacha across last week? Were the Americans to meet Hacha? Speak!"

"I . . . I think so. At least they went to find him."

"Now you are being sensible."

"*Bitte*," Theresa said mechanically. "About Gerhard . . . will he be . . . ?"

"We will get in touch with you. Good night."

When she was sure he had gone, Theresa snatched the telephone and frantically called the Astoria Hotel. Perhaps Herr Loringhoven—why had she never insisted that Gerhard take her to meet him!—could help them. But Herr Loringhoven's suite did not answer.

She tried to get back to sleep. It was impossible.

It was almost five o'clock in the morning, over her fourth cup of yesterday's coffee, when Theresa's shrewd brain began to function again. Now that she thought of it, the police agent had not shown any identification. After all, this was Austria, not Czechoslovakia. . . . That was when the sickening recollection flashed into her mind. Gerhard had mentioned it more than once. Dieter Loringhoven limped.

Theresa fumbled for the telephone. Gerhard . . . Before she could reach it, the phone rang. It was the Vienna city police.

"I was about to call you. . . ."

"One moment, please. We regret to inform you that Herr Mueller's body has been found on the road near Gmünd."

"Body?" Theresa whispered.

"I am sorry. He was murdered. Why were you going to call us?"

When the police swarmed into the Astoria Hotel, it was too late. Loringhoven had already checked out.

They went through the motions of inquiring at the border stations, although they were convinced Dieter Loringhoven had already crossed into Czechoslovakia. They could, of course, expect no help from the Czech police.

They were correct on both accounts.

It was at Loringhoven's telephoned suggestion that the ministry of police in Prague alerted all units for the Budweiser truck. They were to find the truck. They were not to make themselves known. The truck was to be kept under continuous surveillance. Detain no one. But no one was to get away.

The truck was pinpointed on the brief stretch of highway between the Sázava River, a tributary of the Vltava, and the southern outskirts of Prague. A bridge maintenance man, unable to sleep because of the heat in his tin-roofed

shed, had remembered seeing such a truck pass. The driver
of another truck had almost collided with the van outside
Prague when it made a sudden U-turn not thirty meters
ahead of him. It was trapped along thirty kilometers of highway.

The stretch of highway followed low hills hiding the Vltava
gorge, studded with the villas and gardens of the new
bureaucracy; past the gray, drab factories; the rolling fields
with their skeletal poles and wires waiting for the autumn
hops; the higher Bohemian hills with narrow unpaved roads
and footpaths twisting upward through the pines.

Thirty kilometers of highway. With the only satisfactory
hiding place the high, pine forests between the Sázava River
and the suburban factories.

At dawn the army of police, in small groups, moved quietly into the hills.

They had come as far as the southern outskirts of Prague
in darkness. They could not see the lights of the city yet,
for these were hidden by the low, steep hills of the Vltava
gorge, but they had passed a road sign marking the Prague
city limits. They had bowled along for perhaps a mile, over-
taking and passing a slow truck, when Steve suddenly said,
"Where do we start looking for the bum? Prague's a big
city."

Lou Goody shrugged. "You got any ideas?"

"No," Steve admitted. Then he said, "Wait a minute. Turn
around."

"What the hell for? I come this far, Steve, I want a crack
at them ten thousand bucks."

"Turn around, I said. We can hole up in those woods
back there. Then, when it gets light, Andy can drive into
the city and see if he can locate Hacha."

Andy stirred. "Alone?" Goody asked doubtfully.

"Sure, alone. At least he speaks German. All Andy has
to do is set it up for us. If he can find out where Hacha
is, we drive in at night and get it over with."

"How's he gonna drive in?" Goody asked. "In what?"

"That's easy. We find a back road in the woods to hide in.
Then we detach the cab. You and me stay with the vans.
When it gets light Andy goes in the cab."

"Yeah," Goody said, still not convinced.

"Okay, turn back, Lou."

Andy said nothing.

Goody swung the big truck in a U-turn. The truck that they had just passed rumbled down on them.

"Look out!" Andy cried involuntarily.

"Relax, kid. This is the old master at the wheel."

The tail of the second trailer missed the truck by inches. Andy saw the driver shake his fist at them. Lou Goody laughed and stepped on the gas. The factories began to slip by, then the hops fields. Soon they were climbing back into the high hills.

"There's a road, Lou," Steve said.

Lou Goody turned into it. The road was hardpack, just wide enough. Pine boughs cracked and scraped against the sides of the two vans. They went on for half a mile until the dirt road forked. They chose the left, climbed steeply, the truck laboring in low gear.

The road ended in a clearing, in the center of which stood a stone chimney and the charred remains of a cottage.

"What's wrong with right here?"

"It damn well better be right here. There's no place else to go, except back."

Goody was jittery. The woods seemed to bother him. He kept scanning them as if he expected tigers to come bounding into the clearing. Before he would let Steve and Andy out of the cab he insisted on seesawing the truck around to face the way they had come.

"I could use some sleep," Steve said, stretching.

"I could use some grub," Goody said.

"We'll find berries or something in the morning, Lou. With the Czech money we got, Andy can bring us back some groceries after he spots Hacha."

"If he spots him."

If I go, Andy said. But not aloud. Andy Longacre, finger man. The sole Phi Beta Kappa finger man extant. It sounded all wrong. Andy shook his head.

"What you shaking your head about?" Goody growled.

"Was I?"

The gunman came very close. "Look, kid, if you're cooking up another one of your cute ideas, stop cooking. Hear? You're gonna do just like Steve said, or I'll blow your gut clear back to Long Island!"

"Lay off, Lou." Steve sounded very quiet. "Andy'll be all right. Let's get some shuteye."

Andy's last thought as he fell asleep on the hard floor of the van was that he would have to go. For Steve's sake.

20

"The beauty of it is," Minister Otto Zander of the Czechoslovak People's Republic State Police said to Dieter Loringhoven, "Milo Hacha actually has reason to hate old Mydlár. Mydlár, you see, testified against Hacha's father at the trial, and Rudolf Hacha, of course, was executed."

"That is why you brought Milo Hacha back?"

"Precisely. It would be mere bourgeois formalism to claim Rudolf Hacha would have been executed in any event," Zander said. "While now, from the viewpoint of socialist realism, it may be said that Mydlár was responsible for Rudolf Hacha's death. You see?"

Loringhoven merely frowned. He was an *agent provocateur*, not a politician.

"Consider, please," Zander went on in his dry, professional voice. "Mydlár remains a focal point for unrest. Like Rudolf Hacha before him, he is very popular with the masses. He has been stripped of any real power as Minister of the Interior, and though we could try him for treason as Rudolf Hacha was tried, there is a better way. Milo Hacha will assassinate him." Minister Zander smiled. "This has been arranged."

"With Hacha?"

"It has been arranged," the Minister repeated, frowning slightly. Loringhoven did not press the question. "And the Americans?"

"We'll come to them, Comrade. Now. Hacha has slipped across the border from Austria illegally. As far as we are concerned, the government is not involved. Our hands are clean. We know nothing of Hacha's presence until Mydlár's assassination. Then, of course, we are shocked. The masses

howl for the assassin's blood. We are indignant. We give
the martyr a state funeral with full honors. And what is
accomplished? Mydlár, the rallying point for the Social
Democrats, is eliminated, and Milo Hacha, who means nothing, is tried and executed for the murder."

"And the Americans?" Dieter Loringhoven asked again.

"That is where you come in, Herr Loringhoven. The government wishes to keep its hands absolutely clean in this
affair. You will be responsible for returning the Americans
to Austria. For this we will give you whatever police co-
operation you need."

"Have they been found?"

Zander nodded. "Fourteen kilometers north of the Sázava
River. They have been under surveillance since shortly before dawn."

"This limp," Loringhoven said, smiling. "You'd be surprised how it has served me, Herr Minister. An *agent provocateur*, bitter, blaming the government for his injury—"

"I don't understand, Comrade."

"Well, a limp is a defect. I put it to work *for* me. The
Americans—"

"Yes?"

"The Americans are a defect. So we put them to work for
us. For example, if it can be shown that Milo Hacha was
in the pay of foreign, capitalist-imperialist agents?"

"How could you do this?"

"They want to find Milo Hacha but they don't know where
he is. If we led them? If we put rings in their noses and led
them? Suppose—"

Dieter Loringhoven outlined a plan. Minister Otto Zander
was all ears.

"Where's Goody?" Andy asked, climbing down from the
cab.

"We found a stream a couple of hundred yards down the
road. He's getting water. What you doing back here so
soon, kid?"

"Did you want to starve to death?" Andy turned around
and reached up to the high seat of the cab. Grinning, he
tossed Steve two loaves of bread and a big, round, waxy
cheese.

"Where'd you get these?"

"A town called Benesov, back across the river. And that

isn't all." Andy reached into the van again and produced six bottles of beer. "Now say you're sorry I came back!"

"It ain't that, kid. I'm hungry enough to eat a horse, but this don't get us any closer to Milo Hacha."

"First we eat," Andy said. "Go ahead, cut it up." He set the beer on the ground. "Come on, Steve! I'm drooling."

"Listen, Andy. There's something I want to tell you before Lou gets back. If anything happens to me—"

"Nothing's going to happen to you."

"There's a lawyer in Flushing named Philip Dempsey. I gave him a deposition once. Years ago. Life insurance, you might call it. It was so I could get out of the rackets and stay in one piece."

"Why didn't you use it before we left the States?"

"I couldn't. Once they killed Barney I couldn't scare Estelle Street. There was nothing in the deposition could touch her. She had me where she wanted me. But if anything happens to me, you get hold of that deposition and see the county D.A. gets it. I'll feel better knowing. Okay?"

"Okay. But—"

"I know. Nothing's gonna happen to me."

Then they heard Lou Goody tramping up the hill.

Lou's eyes got mean when he saw Andy. He set a heavy gas can full of water on the ground. "I thought you were heading for Prague," he snarled. Then he saw the bread, cheese and beer. He forgot everything else.

A half hour later, Andy climbed back into the detached cab. "How's the gas, Andy?"

"I'll fill up on the way to Prague."

"Good luck!" Then Steve said, "Hold it!" and ran up to the truck, thrusting a Luger in at Andy.

"I don't want—"

"Take it, kid. I'll feel better."

Andy drove down the road with the gun on the seat beside him.

He wished he knew what he was going to do if and when he found Milo Hacha.

The unmarked car drove out from behind some bushes where the dirt road ran into the main highway to Prague. It kept several hundred meters behind Andy. The other police car was half a kilometer ahead of the cab.

Andy saw the trailing car in the side-view mirror, but he

thought nothing of it. He never noticed the lead car at all.

"It is breath-taking, isn't it?" Libusé asked.

Milo Hacha whirled, for she had come up behind him silently. From where he stood in the garden of the Mydlár house he had a magnificent view of the spires of St. Vitus Cathedral, thrusting above the Malá Strana hill, and the massive ramparts of Hradcany Castle.

He nodded. The dark grave girl was an odd one, all right. Since her abrupt outburst the night before she had been the perfect hostess.

"Where is your father?" Hacha asked.

"Arranging everything for tonight, naturally. What are you going to tell them at the Manes Café?"

"Your father is writing my speech."

"Will you deliver it?"

Hacha laughed. "I haven't seen it yet."

He had been told not to make contact with the government. They would get in touch with him. He felt cut off, vulnerable. There was nothing he could do but wait. And tonight, if he said the wrong thing—

Maybe even going to the Manes Café with Vaclav Mydlár would be the wrong thing. If it were a test, as he was half-convinced, how would they expect him to act? Co-operate with the Mydlárs? Publicly disavow them? Remain noncommittal until he was given some official lead to follow?

He heard the back door open and shut. He turned. It was Vaclav Mydlár. The old man's eyes were glittering.

"It is arranged," he said. "All arranged, my boy!"

Milo Hacha nodded with what he hoped looked like enthusiasm.

———◆———

21

"I want to show you something," Minister Zander said. He had not seen Loringhoven since early morning, and both of them had been busy. Zander held up a glossy photograph on stiff paper. "You recognize this? It was taken when he arrived, the one time we had official contact with him."

Dieter Loringhoven studied the photograph. It was a full-face close-up of Milo Hacha staring off into space solemnly.

"Of course. That's Hacha."

Minister Zander raised his voice. "You may come in now."

The office door opened and a man Dieter Loringhoven had never seen before entered. He was in his late thirties, well-built, and had dark hair and broad Slavic cheekbones. "Herr Minister?" he said stiffly.

"Well?" Minister Zander asked Dieter Loringhoven.

"I beg your pardon?"

"He does not resemble Milo Hacha?"

Loringhoven scrutinized the stranger's face. "No. Not at all."

"Good. Very fine." Zander turned to the man. "You may proceed."

Obediently, the Slav turned his back. Dieter Loringhoven saw his hands go to his face. When he faced them again, Dieter Loringhoven gasped. The man now looked incredibly like Milo Hacha.

"Such a subtle thing, facial resemblance," Minister Zander murmured. "An expert touch here, an expert touch there, and you have a double."

"I wouldn't have believed it possible!"

"The basic structure of the face was already similar," Minister Zander said modestly. "But, of course, it is the touches that matter. Also, in this case, it is important that the disguise can be assumed and disposed of in seconds."

He lit a cigar. "In Hacha's case," the Minister continued, "the subtle touches are principally two. First, the eyebrows. Hacha's are darker, thicker. Show him, please."

The stranger rubbed his eyebrows with the fingers of his right hand in a quick movement. He had used a readily removable darkening agent on them. Now his eyebrows were thinner, paler. But he still resembled Milo Hacha.

"Secondly," Minister Zander continued, "Hacha's jaw development is prognathic. Demonstrate, please."

The man opened his mouth and inserted both index fingers. In a moment he had removed four slender cylinders of cotton, of the sort dentists use. And now the resemblance between the stranger and Milo Hacha had ceased to exist.

"Magic!" Loringhoven exclaimed. "Sheer magic."

"It has to be magic, Comrade. One moment he is not Milo Hacha. The next, he is. Then suddenly he must be himself again. Incidentally, when Hacha leaves the Mydlár house tonight to go to the Manes Café, our agents will at once report what he is wearing. You see?"

Dieter Loringhoven nodded in appreciation. Milo Hacha's double bowed and left. Zander leaned forward across his desk. "And you? You, too, have been busy? My men have kept you informed?"

"Yes. One of the Americans is now in Prague—the young one. He parked the truck on the Vaclavské Namesti. He walked. Aimlessly. So far as I know, he is still walking. Twice he has stopped in cafés. He drinks beer. He listens."

"The others?"

"Still in the Sázava hills. Why, I don't know. The one who is here, naturally, doesn't know where to look for Hacha. But he has ears. He has eyes."

"How do you plan to help him?"

"There will be talk in the cafés. Planted, for his benefit. And I visited the office of the Prague *Pravda*."

"*Pravda?*" Minister Zander was clearly surprised. Dieter Loringhoven was pleased to have the shoe on the other foot. "Does he understand the language—?"

Loringhoven shrugged. "He goes into the cafés along the Vaclavské and listens. Why should one of them enter Prague and the other two remain behind?"

"Because this one speaks Czech and they do not!" Minister Zander said, delighted.

"Czech? That's not likely. But German, perhaps. So, for the afternoon's German-language edition of Prague *Pravda*, there is to be one special copy printed."

"Yes?" said Minister Zander.

"That copy will get into the hands of the American."

A smile of appreciation spread over the Minister's face.

It was insufferably hot in midafternoon along the Vaclavské Namesti.

Drab crowds drifted along, but the broad avenue was almost empty of motor traffic. A tram rattled by, an occasional horse-drawn wagon, an automobile.

At first Andy experienced the disconcerting certainty that everyone was staring at him suspiciously. But he soon noticed that the crowds were too apathetic to care about anything but their sweltering misery.

He had dropped in at three cafés after parking the truck in the almost empty municipal lot at one end of the Vaclavské Namesti. There had been much beer-drinking and talk, in both Czech and German, but none of it mentioned the name Milo Hacha.

Still, he could think of no other way to pick up Hacha's trail. He would give himself until nightfall—and then what? Would Steve or Lou Goody take no for an answer?

Worse still, what if he *did* learn Hacha's whereabouts? Report failure anyway? Finger the repatriated Czech for them? The way it shaped up, Andy thought glumly—either condemn an innocent man to sudden death or send his own brother to the chair.

He stopped thinking about it abruptly. He was hot and thirsty and tired. He decided to try one more café along the Namesti before returning to the hills of Old Prague across the river.

Andy passed another small café, stopped and retraced his steps. It might as well be this one as any other. On the wide sidewalk stood a double row of tables shielded from the sun by trees. He sat down at one of the two unoccupied tables outside. The other, adjacent to it, was soon occupied by two men in double-breasted suits.

A waiter came over, and Andy ordered beer. The waiter took another order, also given in German, for white wine at the next table. Andy sat back and drank his beer thirstily when it came, ordered another, and a third. Helmut's wallet had contained about twenty dollars' worth of Czech currency. He had had to have the truck's gas tank filled on the way to Prague. He had used more for the bread, cheese and beer. He would have to go easy with what was left. He decided, regretfully, not to order a fourth beer.

"You are excited?" one of the men at the next table asked the other, giving him a cynical grin.

"*Ja, ja,* a little."

"You expect miracles from this man?"

Andy listened to the exchange automatically. He was far more interested in a hysterical argument in the street, where two bicyclists had just collided.

The second man sipped his wine. "After all," he said, "he is his father's son."

"Even the father wasn't a worker of miracles." The cynic laughed. "He has yet to rise from the dead."

"Well, I don't suppose we can expect much from the son, but the fact is, the government has called him to an important post and allows him to meet tonight with the old Social Democrats—"

Andy's heart jumped. He found himself gripping his beer stein in a death clutch.

"*Ach,* we'll see. How is Maria?"

"The heat. She hates the summer. You are going tonight?"

"And why should I go?"

"Because the man has a magic name, I tell you. Anything can happen."

"I am no Social Democrat, my friend."

"Even so. They'll be in the Malá Strana in force tonight."

"Maybe that is what the government wants to happen."

"Do you really think so, Emil?"

"What did Rudolf Hacha ever do for the people? He couldn't even keep himself from the hangman."

"Times have changed. Well, I must be going."

The two men finished their wine, dropped some coins on the table and rose. They shook hands and separated on the sidewalk, swallowed by the crowds.

Andy paid for his beer quickly. He had one of them in view; it might pay to follow him. He had not taken three steps when a hand came down heavily on his shoulder. He whirled. It was the waiter.

"*Mein Herr,*" the waiter said, "you have not paid enough." He shoved the restaurant check in front of Andy's face.

Andy dropped three more coins into his hand, not sure of their denomination. The waiter grunted, and Andy hurried on.

After half a block he knew it was useless. His man had disappeared.

At the corner Andy paused to look down the street to his left. It was a narrow, cobbled lane sloping to the river. Beyond it he could see the stone arches of the Charles Bridge and, higher up, above the Malá Strana, the solid massiveness of Hradcany Castle.

He turned the corner.

That was where the newsdealer, an old woman in boots,

was standing. As he was about to pass her, she thrust a newspaper at him. *"Pravda?"* she said. *"Pravda?"*

Andy glanced at it. What luck! The paper was in German.
He bought it.

* * *

22

Andy arrived early, with the four-sheet, tabloid-sized newspaper folded in his pocket and the Luger galling weight
against his bare skin. He sat down in the smaller of the
Manes Café's two rooms; it sported a bar, a few tables,
leather-covered sofas along three walls and above them, life-
sized portraits of Lenin, Stalin and Klement Gottwald.

The second room, with the magnificent view, was closed
to the public for tonight. That was where, according to the
newspaper in Andy's pocket, the Social Democrats would
greet the son of their hero.

By nine-thirty the smaller room was crowded, although
individual groups rarely contained more than two or three
men. There were several couples. But except for Andy, there
was only one other patron sitting alone over a beer. This was
a big, well-built and good-looking man in his late thirties,
with broad Slavic cheekbones. He was wearing a gray suit,
a shirt open at the collar and no tie.

Then the first large group of Social Democrats came in
and were ushered into the larger room. The waiter began
scurrying back and forth, holding high steins of foaming
beer and bottles of red and white wine. Before long, two
more groups arrived and went into the large room after the
others.

Milo Hacha was with the fourth and final group. Andy
knew it was Hacha from the way the others deferred to
him. His immediate entourage consisted of an old man with
twinkling eyes and a grave, pretty girl, rather thin, who
hardly spoke and did not smile at all. Behind them were a
dozen men, most of them past middle age.

They passed by Andy's table.

So that's Milo Hacha, Andy thought.

The man he and Steve had crossed the Atlantic to find for Estelle Street. The man they had tracked halfway through Europe.

The man who's responsible, Andy thought with a grimace, for the lousy and inescapable trap I find myself in.

Hacha was tall yet compactly built. He walked with the grace of a man who has kept himself in shape at a time when men of his age were beginning to slump here and there. His face was Slavic and hard, with the slightly lumpy look of an old pro prizefighter. He was wearing a gray suit and an open-throated shirt, like the similarly Slavic-looking man drinking alone nearby.

Somehow, seeing the man in the flesh at last was an anti-climax. He was attractive enough, radiating a male magnetism that women like Trudy Ohlendorf would find irresistible. But in his mind Andy had built up a portrait of a superman, and the reality struck him as far from that.

In the few moments he had to observe Hacha at close range, Andy tried to see in him the hero, the daring under-cover fighter for human liberty, the giant of causes legends sprang up about. But he couldn't. In fact, there was some-thing about Hacha that kept niggling at Andy in a sort of plea for recognition. Possibly it had something to do with the man's nervousness. There was a wet gloss to his forehead; he kept smiling almost mechanically at those greeting him. The superman of the Milo Hacha legend did not sweat for emotional reasons or have to force his smiles.

Suddenly Andy saw what was really bothering him. He doubted his conclusion even as it occurred to him. There was something phony about Hacha.

But I'm not here to make a character-analysis of the guy, Andy thought.

The question immediately popped into his mind, just why *am* I here? I'm supposed to locate Hacha. I've located him. All I have to do is get up, go back to the hills, give Steve and Goody the lowdown, and my part is finished. Even if I have to guide them back here, my part is finished. Then why don't I get up and go?

Because I can't, he answered himself, I just can't. I'm immobilized here like an insect stuck on flypaper.

He called desperately for another beer.

An ambulatory Hungarian violinist was playing a marching song Andy did not recognize. The Social Democrats in the other room broke into enthusiastic applause.

Through the doorway Andy could see about half the big room—a wall of windows, panes slanted open to let in the night air; a section of the wide horseshoe table gay with many flickering candles; the shifting planes and curves in the animated faces seated around it.

As Andy shifted in his chair he felt with surprise the dig of the Luger against his body. He had forgotten the gun. Was this a reminder that here he was, and there Hacha was, and all he had to do was walk into the other room and shoot the guy through the head? That would solve everybody's problem. But even as the thought passed through his mind, Andy knew it was absurd. He could never do it. All he could do was sit here in the Manes Café, pinned to his chair.

He became aware of a disturbance behind him. He turned and saw a couple attempting to leave. They had gotten as far as the doorway, where a man blocked their path. The woman spoke to her escort, tugging at his arm. He raised his voice. The man in their way asked a question. Apparently it was a rhetorical question, for he shook his own head without waiting for an answer.

The man and woman came back into the room and sat down. ". . . go if we want to," the man said loudly. "We haven't done anything."

"Fool!" the woman snapped at him. "Don't you recognize the police when you see them?"

They spoke in German. Andy glanced at the man who had stopped them. He was leaning against the doorframe, his eyes never still. A policeman? Apparently they—whoever "they" were—weren't going to let anyone leave the Manes Café until this was over.

And suppose, Andy thought, suppose they decided to check everybody's papers?

Or search the patrons?

Andy inhaled noiselessly and ordered another beer.

The issue was out of his hands. He was stuck here. Exactly like the fly.

". . . although the government will tell you," Vaclav Mydlár spoke over his wineglass, "there is no relationship between a father and son except by biological accident"— here there was laughter— we have at least this fact to go by:

of his own free will, the biological accident has returned to us."

More laughter, some applause, but no spontaneous demonstration. That made Milo Hacha, sitting uncomfortably at old Mydlár's right, feel better. He didn't want a spontaneous demonstration. He didn't want to be carried anywhere, on any tide. Except toward the approval of the government.

". . . fitting that the Manes Café is the scene of this meeting. I need not remind you of the history of this famous tavern, nor of the misery some of its—ah, alumni—have brought to Europe. But we remember misery and we tend to forget triumph. Thus it was not misery in 1848 when . . ."

Hacha looked around the big horseshoe table. In the candlelight he could not see faces sharply. But there was no sound in the room now except the sound of Vaclav Mydlár's clear voice. The audience was attentive; some seemed rapt. Hacha, a stranger alike to politics and historical meanings, felt completely out of his depth. All he knew was that safety lay with the strong, and these were the weak.

". . . two traditional ways to revolution in Eastern Europe. The first, but the way we here reject categorically, was the way of Hitler and—yes, face it, we are here because of this tonight—the way of the Bolsheviks. This is also the way of violence. Of violent revolution. Of the club and the gun and terror in the night. But there is another way, my friends, there is the way of the moderates. Of us Social Democrats. For if the will to power of the many is ever to take precedence over the will to power of the few, then violent revolution must be shunned. This, my friends, is just as true under totalitarian . . ."

The speech, now, was forgotten. So were the dimly-seen faces around the table. For Milo Hacha had the message he had been waiting for.

The note which the headwaiter had just brought him read: "A representative of the Ministry of the Interior wishes to see you in the other room. *At once.*" The note was unsigned.

Hurriedly reading the note a second time, Hacha felt his elation dissolve in an acid fear. The message he had been waiting for? Perhaps it was . . . reverse. The reverse! It was a test, as he had suspected from the beginning, and he had failed. He had done exactly the wrong thing. He should have refused to attend this stupid meeting. . . .

Hacha rose abruptly. All the damned nearsighted Socialist

eyes were staring at him in bewilderment. Old Mydlár had stopped in the middle of a sentence; his eyes were the most bewildered of all. Libusé Mydlár was half out of her chair.

"You must excuse me," Hacha said curtly. "I have had an important message."

Libusé began to whisper something, placed her hand on his arm. But Hacha pulled away, went to the doorway and through it.

Andy saw the Slavic-featured man dressed like Milo Hacha crook his finger at the headwaiter. The headwaiter came over and stooped deferentially over the man's table. The man scribbled something on a slip of paper. He folded it once and handed it to the headwaiter with a decisive-sounding word in Czech.

The headwaiter immediately walked into the large room.

Andy watched the Slav at the table. He was glancing directly at the police agent guarding the door. The police agent nodded slightly, as if a signal or an order had been communicated to him.

Andy looked over into the big room. The headwaiter was handing the folded paper to Milo Hacha with a bow.

What the hell was going on here?

". . . the Gomulka government at the outset," Vaclav Mydlár said, amazed at the unexpected power in his voice, "had the right idea. But what happened soon afterward in Hungary frightened the Poles. Tragically, what could have been the embryo of a true Social Democratic movement in Poland, a movement by evolution, not revolution, away from the Bolsheviks—this movement under a now-frightened Gomulka aborted, and Gomulka became an unwilling tool of the Bolsheviks, afraid for his life."

Vaclav Mydlár paused to sip from his wineglass. Amazingly, Milo Hacha had become unimportant to him. His voice had not even faltered after he recovered from the surprise of Hacha's sudden departure. It was as if all the years of Mydlár's old, tired life had been pointing to this instant in space and time.

". . . but slowly. For although the heavy foot of the Red horde lies on the neck of Europe, even the empire of an Alexander, Hitler, Lenin does not endure. It, too, crumbles under the erosion of time. This, my friends, is our legacy. This is our hope, our future. Let history say—"

Then Professor Mydlár stopped. Milo Hacha was striding back into the room. Purposefully. Not the indecisive Hacha who had spent several nervous days at the Mydlár home. This was a new Hacha.

A Hacha with a gun in his hand.

People all around the table, wondering at Mydlár's sudden pause, turned in their chairs to see what had stopped him. Mouths fell open. They sat frozen in their twisted attitudes.

Oddly, Vaclav Mydlár was now looking not at the approaching gun, but at his daughter Libusé. Libusé, too, sat frozen. But in her dark, intelligent face a bitter knowledge was imbedded in the horror.

So this is the end of me, old Mydlár thought in perfect calmness.

Then he heard two bursts of sound.

Then he heard nothing and felt nothing. He was aware only of the ceiling far, far above him.

Libusé's face came glazed and tender between him and the ceiling. Libusé . . . That was good.

"Go," he heard his own distant voice. "You have always wished to go, my beloved. You have stayed only for my sake. But now I no longer matter and you must go, Libusé. Where you can speak out. Where they will listen. Libusé, where are you? Libusé . . ."

When Milo Hacha heard the two shots he sprang to his feet. "Sit down," Minister Zander said. "It will probably take some time for you to grasp the thought that you are under arrest." He sounded amused. "Meanwhile, sit down."

Hacha mechanically obeyed. Then he saw a man darting out of the banquet room. Hacha thought, where have I seen him before?

Suddenly he knew. Why, in the mirror. He's me! . . . A double. *A double.*

The double turned his back, putting his hands to his face. When he turned around he was no longer Milo Hacha, but another man.

"The gun," Minister Zander said sharply, holding out his manicured hand. "Good. Now get out, quickly."

The man fled.

Hacha sat stupidly.

Minister Zander looked around the room. All but a dozen or so people at the tables were police agents. Dieter Loringhoven was going over to the young American's table, where the boy sat gripping an empty glass. He was very pale.

Zander shrugged. These few must be detained, arrested probably. Or, safest of all, quietly disposed of. It would not be difficult. The American boy was a complication, true, perhaps requiring a more elaborate solution. . . .

The Minister turned in some annoyance at a sudden scramble behind him.

Milo Hacha was struggling with three agents. Then, astoundingly, the three agents were flying through the air. And Hacha, with incredible speed, was running into the banquet room. "No!" he was shouting. "No! I am Milo Hacha! *I am Milo Hacha!*"

It was exactly like the dream Hacha had dreamed, over and over, since the war, of trying in vain to persuade the faceless people of his identity, his good intentions, his purity and compassion, while they tore him to pieces.

Some struck him. Some clawed at his clothes. His arms were being seized. His legs.

"Murderer!"

"Traitor!"

"It's a mistake! I tell you it was not I who—!"

The girl, Libusé, was screaming in his ear. Blows, blows rained on his face, his body, his soul. He tried to strike back, to kick, to penetrate the wall between them. . . .

Suddenly he was free, jumping over a heap of them where they had tumbled one another in their unorganized rage to get at him. But where to run? They were all between him and the doorway. He retreated slowly, talking, pleading, explaining, and almost fell over something soft and still. It was Vaclav Mydlár's body, still on the floor.

"No, see, I was outside. You all saw how they sent for me. They arrested me. I was helpless. It was someone else who came in here with the gun. You must not think . . . a trick . . . the police . . ."

But they heard nothing, as in the dream. They were stalking him now in a body, slowly, without expression. He kept backing up, talking, talking, until he could back up no more. Hacha wiped the blood from his eyes, crouching a little, waiting, talking, pleading.

A wineglass shattered against his cheek. Then they were upon him.

They picked Milo Hacha up—he was still talking, still telling them the simple truth of his innocence—and they flung him through the great window of the banquet room. He fell and fell in the warm bloody darkness watching Hradcany Castle spin and fly away until he fell no more.

In the vanguard of the people shouting and struggling through the overwhelmed police agents in the smaller room was Libusé Mydlár. She was thinking with great clarity as her slender body was being pushed and pummeled and propelled toward the narrow passageway to the staircase. I have to escape, now, tonight, or I never shall. He is dead and it was his dying wish. If not tonight, then never, for surely Hacha was in the pay of the government, and if I am not gone by morning they will come looking for me.

The words of her father's speech rang in Libusé's memory like cathedral bells proclaiming victory. That was his legacy to mankind, and she must deliver it.

Minister Zander sat in the wreckage of the Manes Café thinking hard.

One tear-gas bomb, he was thinking, just one and I'd have had them all. But there were no tear-gas bombs. Who could have anticipated a flock of sheep turning on their dogs?

Worst blunder of all, Zander mused, was allowing Milo Hacha, fool that he was, to offer himself as a sacrifice on the altar of self-justification. He should have been spirited away the moment he left the banquet room in response to the note. As it was, he was dead, and of what use was a dead man at a State trial?

I don't even have the American, the Minister thought sourly. Of course he took advantage of the confusion to escape with the sheep.

Zander glanced over at the table that the young American had occupied. Dieter Loringhoven was standing there, supporting himself with one hand on the table top, the other dabbing at his mouth with a bloodstained handkerchief. Another fool. Whom could one depend on!

Some police agents appeared, gripping the arms of half a dozen captured sheep. A fine haul! the Minister thought. Of course the girl, Mydlár's daughter, was not among them. Nor the American . . .

Four cylinders of cotton, Zander thought. And some eye shadow and a few other tricks. That was it, naturally. The man can be found, I know where to find *him*, at least. Several months in a dungeon, a little scientific starvation, the un-failing conversion of the brain to believe its assigned identity and its guilt—that was child's play.

But suddenly Minister Zander realized that he needed more than a resurrected Milo Hacha to repair the damage. His own skin was in peril now.

If I can give them an additional scapegoat . . .

"Lieutenant," Minister Zander said.

A rather battered police agent ran over and stood stiffly at attention.

"You will arrest that man," Minister Zander pointed to Dieter Loringhoven.

Part SIX

Andy

———————◆———————

23

When he had fought his way to the street, Andy broke through the crowd surrounding Milo Hacha's body, intent on nothing but getting away—fast. His knuckles, where they had smashed in some of Dieter Loringhoven's teeth, were bleeding profusely, but the hell with that now.

Then he stopped. A woman ahead of him was trying to shoulder her way through the throngs on the sidewalk; she was biting her lip, holding her side. It was the dark, pretty girl he had seen upstairs with Milo Hacha and the old man who had been shot.

Andy lunged and grabbed her arm. She turned fiercely, ready to scratch his face. "Wait, wait," he said in German. "I know who you are and I'm trying to get away, too. Are you hurt badly?"

"No. . . . My ribs. Bruised . . ." Her eyes were wild.

"Have you a car?"

"Yes. But—"

"Where is it? On this street?" Meanwhile he was hurrying her down the hill, toward the river.

"No, no, this way," the girl panted, rounding the corner. "The third car—you must help me—get away—" She stopped dead in her tracks, her eyes widening. Then she edged into the shadow of the building.

The third car was a long black sedan. a Russian-built Zis.

And there, leaning against the front left door, stood a man in uniform.

A police uniform.

"Take it easy," Andy said in a low voice. He pulled a cigarette from his pocket and searched as if for a match. "Do you have a match, dearest?" he asked loudly. "No, of course, you don't smoke. Why can't I remember?" He laughed and said, "Perhaps this policeman . . ."

He walked leisurely toward the policeman, who was watching them suspiciously. The man's hand went to his holster.

"Do you happen to have a match, officer?" Andy asked in German. He was still poking around in his clothing.

The man said something sharp in Czech. Libusé screamed, *"He knows!"* and Andy was astonished at the speed with which the Luger jumped into his hand and went up and came down with a sickening thud on the policeman's head. The man's eyes turned over and he slid peacefully to the sidewalk, falling over on his face.

I did it, Andy thought, appalled. I really did it. He had felt a kind of leaping satisfaction at the impact of his fist against Loringhoven's mouth in the café, but this . . . a gun . . . The poor guy might even be dead. . . .

He felt the girl shaking his arm wildly. "Come, come, we cannot stand here!" she was saying, over and over.

"Oh . . . Yes." He snatched open the car door and she scrambled in. "Wait. The key! Do you have the key?"

"What?" She sounded dazed.

"The ignition key!"

". . . driver. Police driver. My father was an official of the government, you see. . . ."

Andy knelt and frantically began to search the policeman.

"You must hurry. Please," the girl said in a dead voice.

He found a ring of keys and ran around the car and jumped in behind the wheel. It was like an old-time movie. He kept jabbing keys into the ignition lock and none of them would fit. People were screaming and running past the corner, chased by police agents, and Andy expected the fallen policeman to be spotted at any moment. When one of the keys slid into the lock he found himself saying silently, thank you, thank you, thank you.

The sedan jerked away from the curb. Andy headed it down the hill toward the Charles Bridge.

"South of Trebon in the Bohemian forest," Libusé said in the same dead way. "Who are you?"

"My name is Andy."

"The border there. They can't guard every meter of the pine forest at night."

"I beg pardon?"

"The gasoline."

Andy was bewildered. She did jump around so. Must be shock. "What did you say?"

"Is there enough gasoline?"

But they were rolling across the cobbles of the Charles Bridge now, and Andy quietly put the Luger in his lap. There was a police booth at the other end of the bridge. To his amazement, the policeman stepped aside, saluting, to let them pass.

Andy almost laughed as he released his breath. He had forgotten. This was an official car. Cosy!

"Gasoline, gasoline," the girl was saying.

"What?" Andy glanced, startled, at the gas gauge. The tank was almost empty.

"We have lost," she said with a childlike sigh. "I think I knew this from the beginning. We cannot stop for gasoline; all stations will have been alerted. But you have been so very kind. I wish I knew your name."

Andy took one hand from the wheel to shake her. "Snap out of it!" he said in English. "I mean," he added in German, "my name is Andy—Andy—"

"Andy," she said, as if pleased.

"And we are not lost yet, Fräulein."

"No?" she said dreamily.

He told her about the truck and where it was parked. "How do I get there from here?"

She seemed to come to life. She sat up straighter and there was awareness in her voice as she gave him directions.

Andy left the sedan a block from the municipal parking lot as a precaution. He took Libusé's arm and they strolled over to the almost deserted lot and got into the cab. Andy started the engine, turned on the lights and drove out.

An ordinary-looking car drove out a half-minute later. The two policemen staked out in it had watched the American with some girl or other get into the truck and drive away. They had made no attempt to interfere because their orders were specific: follow the truck.

They followed the truck.

"He should of been back," Lou Goody growled. He was hungry and irritable. They had long since finished the last of the bread, cheese and beer.

"All *right*, Lou. But what's the use of beefing? We'll just have to wait," Steve said.

"What's he trying to pull?"

"He's not trying to pull anything. He'll be back."

"Oh, yeah? When? You know what time it is? It's damn near one-thirty."

Steve ground his teeth in silence. Lou Goody was worrying because they hadn't yet found Milo Hacha. That no longer bothered Steve. He was afraid for Andy. It's all my fault, he kept groaning to himself, this whole nutty caper. And on top of everything else, to let Andy go all by himself into the damn city of Red wolves . . . If anything's happened to him . . .

If Andy gets back here in one piece, I'll square it with him. If it takes the rest of my life and every crooked dime I've got, I'll square it with him. . . .

"Listen," Goody said suddenly. "Hear something?"

Steve listened. It was the sound of an engine, laboring. Laboring up the hill!

"It must be Andy," Steve cried. "By God, he's made it!"

"Maybe it is and maybe it isn't," Goody said. He took out his Luger.

They waited.

Headlights suddenly pierced the darkness around the last hairpin turn. The engine sounded as if it were picking up speed. Steve started running.

"Steve, you damn fool! What if it ain't—?"

"It is!" Steve shouted exultantly.

The truck stopped and Andy climbed down from the cab.

"Kid, kid," Steve said, feeling Andy all over. "You're okay. You made it. What happened to you?" he said sharply. "You look as if you've been through a cement mixer!"

"It's a long story," Andy said tiredly. "By the way, Steve, I'm not alone. There's a girl in the cab."

"Girl?" Steve said stupidly. "What girl?"

"We'd better hurry. We'll be crowded, but there's that shelf behind the driver's seat—"

"A dame?" Goody snarled. "This is one hell of a time to start playing with dames! What about Hacha? Did you find the bum? Come on, kid, talk!"

"Hacha's dead."

Goody gaped.

But Steve said in a strangled voice, "Andy, you mean you—?"

"No," Andy said. "I didn't kill anyone but a policeman—maybe. God, I hope not, I hope not. . . . Look, we can't stay here. We've got to get going. . . ."

When the truck trundled out of the dirt road onto the main highway and headed south, away from Prague, the two men in the unmarked Prague police car waited a short time in the bushes where they had been hiding. Then they pulled out onto the highway and followed the truck.

Minister Zander did not think of the Americans until later that night, in his office, when the report came in that their truck had left the municipal parking lot and had driven out of Prague.

The Minister had been enjoying a moment of self-congratulation. All things considered, he had done not badly, not badly at all. A round dozen Social Democrats had been caught. From them the names of all those who had attended the meeting at the café could easily be extracted. In brief interviews with three of them, Minister Zander had expressed his horrified shock over Vaclav Mydlár's assassination by Milo Hacha.

When the substitute Milo Hacha and Dieter Loringhoven had been properly prepared for their trial, they would readily admit their guilt. Hacha would explain that he had killed old Mydlár in revenge for his part in Milo's father's death; Loringhoven would reveal himself as the clever *agent provocateur* who had been in the pay of the capitalist-imperialists all along.

Indeed, the Minister thought, he had not done badly. Mydlár was out of the way; and while the government could be indignant over his assassination, the Social Democrats, shorn of their leader, would become impotent.

A top-level case, no doubt about it. The Premier himself would surely be interested. The Minister especially liked his inspiration about Loringhoven, who had masterminded the spiriting of Hacha into the country. Loringhoven gave the case that touch of perfection. . . .

Only, there were those Americans.

The Americans were the loose end. Loose ends were intolerable; indeed, one might unravel the entire beautiful fabric. He must have the Americans, so that they could be brainwashed into admitting publicly that they had been Dieter Loringhoven's confederates.

"What time is it?"

"Almost three-forty, Commandant."

"Alert the Austrian border stations," Minister Zander said. "Stop the truck at the border. Bring them back."

It was the only direction in which the Americans could flee.

"The town we passed through was Trebon," Libusé said. "We are close to the border now. We will enter Austria near Gmünd."

"In this truck?" Andy asked.

"No, on foot. I will tell you when to stop. There is a barbed-wire fence and there are patrols. But it is not difficult. They would need a million men to guard the border thoroughly. The Reds have learned that."

"What're you two yapping about?" Lou Goody snapped.

"We're going to park the truck and walk," Andy said.

He stared ahead along the winding road, the dark pine forest slipping by swiftly on either side. They passed a clearing, a farmhouse, then more woodland.

"I saw a map once," Libusé said. "Ahead, on the right, two kilometers, there will be another farmhouse. There the road turns sharply west. Then we stop and walk, Andy. It is not far."

They passed the farm. Somewhere, far away, a dog barked. A plowed field, the furrows black in the moonlight. Then more pine forest, and the road curved to the right.

"Here," Libusé Mydlár said. "In fifteen minutes we'll be in Austria."

"I don't like leaving the truck," Goody said.

But when Steve barked at him he pulled up at the side of the road and they all got out. The air smelled wet. It was the first cool night Andy remembered since leaving Switzerland.

"Hold it," Goody said. "You hear something?"

They heard it. A car, coming along the road, fast. Then, from the other direction, from the border, shouts.

"Quickly!" Libusé cried. She darted toward the woods. Suddenly she stopped.

At the limit of vision, in the moonlight, Steve thought he saw the border shed against the brighter night sky and figures of booted men running down the road in their direction.

Lou Goody dived toward the truck. The rest of them were frozen in the shadow of the woods.

"*Halt!*" a heavy voice yelled. (The word is the same in German and English.)

Lou Goody kept going.

"We can still get away," Libusé called urgently in German. "But you must hurry, Andy. Don't stand there to die!"

"You run," Andy said to her gently. "I have to stay here."

"No!" Libusé cried.

Goody had clawed the truck door open. Without warning Steve plunged ahead of him into the truck. Goody scrambled in after him, already slipping the gears into reverse.

"Get out of here, kid!" Steve shouted from the cab. "Go with the girl!"

"No! Steve! Wait—"

The truck shot backward down the road, engine grinding as it pitched from side to side, picking up speed.

At that instant the police car sped around the curve.

Here's your chance, kid, Steve thought. Here's your chance. Lou Goody fought him for control of the wheel, but he was not quick enough. There was a grinding, metal-rending crash.

What was left of Lou Goody went through the roof of the truck cab. Steve's body was flung fifteen yards through the sprung door.

Libusé tugged at Andy's arm and he followed her numbly into the woods. "Come," she urged. "Please. You must."

But he waited, and she waited with him, crouched in the bushes, until the border guards arrived. Only when they found Steve's body and Andy heard one of them say he was dead, did he move again.

In less than fifteen minutes they came to the barbed-wire

fence. They climbed through the strands and kept walking until they reached the road, the Austrian road, that led to Gmünd.

At Gmünd they surrendered to the Austrian border guards.

———◆———

24

From Andy Longacre's diary:

He must have thought it was our only chance, mine and Libusé Mydlár's. Maybe it was. I like to think so.

I've seen Philip Dempsey. I've delivered Steve's deposition to the D.A. in Long Island County. It made all the headlines and for the last few days they've been rounding up people nobody knew were hoodlums.

So much has happened so fast. Or maybe that's because Steve's gone. Sometimes I think, he's still alive and we're going to sit down over a beer and talk about what happened.

Libusé Mydlár's in England. I got a letter from her. She's all excited about a book she's going to write. About her father and the setup in Czechoslovakia.

I can't help thinking about her, because thinking about her reminds me of something else and someone else. Trudy, and what she once wrote to me. Because the last time I saw Libusé Mydlár, she was in despair. I didn't know if she'd ever snap out of it, but apparently she did. What was it Trudy wrote? I wish I had her letter, but I think I remember it: "Masterpieces are not produced from love of life. They are produced from despair."

So maybe Libusé Mydlár will have her masterpiece and maybe it will be the blow she wants to strike against the ugly thing that cost her father his life.

I keep thinking of Milo Hacha. I think, finally, I know what it was about the idea of him that got me. He was a drifter. He was foot-loose. He didn't care about anyone but himself. He spent all his life running away from something without knowing what he was running away from.

The way I see it, he was running away from himself. Funny, I never even spoke to him.

Right now I've got work to do. I've seen Philip Dempsey about another matter—Barney Street's estate. With Estelle Street dead Dempsey thinks there's a good chance it can be left to Milo Hacha's daughter in Holland, or at least part of it.

If the details can be worked out, I'll bring her the good news myself. Probably on the way I'll stop in England and see Libusé Mydlár.

Meanwhile, I'd better attend to my application for that fellowship out West.

I think Steve would have liked that.

Other SIGNET Books You'll Enjoy

☐ **KRUMNAGEL by Peter Ustinov.** KRUMNAGEL asks the all-important question: Can an honest, law-loving, crime-hating police chief overcome the forces of weak-kneed liberalism and stuffy courts of law that want to stop him from using his gun as it was meant to be used—that is to say, every time he feels the urge? "Devastatingly funny!"—*Publishers Weekly.* "Krumnagel is the anti-hero of the year!"—*Harper's* (#Y5238—$1.25)

☐ **FUZZ by Ed McBain.** A homemade bomb, a couple of fun-loving youngsters and an ingenious extortion scheme add up to big excitement. Now a major motion picture from United Artists, starring Burt Reynolds, Racquel Welch, and Yul Brynner. (#T5151—75¢)

☐ **HAIL, HAIL, THE GANG'S ALL HERE by Ed McBain.** In this 87th Precinct Mystery all of Ed McBain's detectives come together for the first time and they're all kept hopping. Some of the stories are violent, some touching, some ironic, but all are marked by the masterful McBain touch . . . the "gang" has never been better. (#T5063—75¢)

☐ **THE FAMILY by Leslie Waller.** A marvelous blend of high finance, illicit romance and the Mafia makes THE FAMILY compelling reading. (#Y4024—$1.25)

☐ **SAM THE PLUMBER by Henry Zeiger.** The explosive real-life saga of Mafia chieftain, Simone Rizzo—taken from thirteen volumes of verbatim conversation overheard by an FBI "bug." (#Q4290—95¢)

THE NEW AMERICAN LIBRARY, INC.,
P.O. Box 999, Bergenfield, New Jersey 07621

Please send me the SIGNET BOOKS I have checked above. I am enclosing $_____(check or money order—no currency or C.O.D.'s). Please include the list price plus 25¢ a copy to cover handling and mailing costs. (Prices and numbers are subject to change without notice.)

Name_____

Address_____

City_____ State_____ Zip Code_____

Allow at least 3 weeks for delivery